wordhoard

ANGLO-SAXON STORIES

WORT

JILL
PATON WALSH
and
KEVIN
CROSSLEY-HOLLAND

ꞏOARꟼ

NGLO-SAXON STORIES

MACMILLAN

Published by
MACMILLAN AND CO LTD
Little Essex Street London W C 2
and also at Bombay Calcutta and Madras
Macmillan South Africa (Publishers) Pty Ltd Johannesburg
The Macmillan Company of Australia Pty Ltd Melbourne
The Macmillan Company of Canada Ltd Toronto
Gill & Macmillan Ltd Dublin

Printed in Great Britain by
W & J MACKAY & CO LTD, CHATHAM

for Caroline and for Tony

For Children

Contents

The Woodwose

The oldest man, a leader of men,
answered; he unlocked the wordhoard.

CEALLA looked up from the new furrows he was planting with winter corn, and frowned as the children came running from the golden wood, calling to each other, and to him, in high screaming voices.

"Where's the firewood?" he demanded, seeing their empty hands.

"We couldn't get it," said Wulfrun, lifting her thin face to him, and returning his gaze, unashamed.

Cealla's temper snapped. "By all the gods, you brats deserve a flogging!" he cried. "I and your mother, Wulfrun, and your mother and father, Beorn, and yours, and yours, bend over plough and harrow in the fields day after day, slaving to bring in food for your greedy gullets, and you, feckless and useless idlers will not even bring kindling for the fires!"

The little group of children fell silent, moved closer to one another.

"You will remember one day, with bitterness in your hearts, the times when you had nothing to do but go gathering in the woods!" he lamented, for his back and arms were aching.

"There was a bear there," said Totta, the youngest boy, "and so we were frightened and ran home."

"Freya strikes dumb those who lie," said Cealla, his anger cold now. "Go back and bring wood, or the supper pots will be cold."

But the children stood still. They shrank a little from his anger, but they did not move back towards the wood. They glanced over their shoulders at the line of russet branches, and the dark tunnels between the tree-trunks, where the wood began, and they stayed still.

"There *was* a bear," said Beorn, the oldest of them. "We found its smelly lair, and then it came and chased us, and it was black, and shaggy, and it roared at us."

"Get you gone!" cried Cealla. "Do I not know that there have been no bears in these woods in our time or our fathers' time? I shall drive you to work with my belt across your backs if you take not your lying tongues out of my reach!"

The children fled, each one running for his own parents' door. Only Wulfrun, who had nowhere to run to, since Cealla was her father, was left.

"But there *was* a bear. I saw it," she said.

Cealla put down the basket of seed corn, and looked at his daughter. He and his wife bewailed the girl's failings every day, but they had never had cause to call her a liar before. He sent her home to his wife, and went to find Offa his neighbour.

The story went round the village quickly, for it was only a small place. The men left the sowing and gathered to talk at the end of the village, where there was a roughly-hewn wooden boar's head set up on a pole to bring luck to their councils.

"There are two hours left until dark," said Readda, who was the richest man. "We had best go now, and see."

They took nets and spears with them, and Readda, who had

an iron sword, went to fetch it, and brought also his son, Totta, to tell them where to look.

Cealla had two fierce hunting dogs which he had caught and tamed himself. They were fearless against wild boar, and might even face a bear, if bear there really was. He called them to heel, and went with the other men.

"He was up by the height of the wood," said Totta. "We were playing by the Giants' Wall, and then we went through the gate in it, where we have never been before, and then he was there."

"What is the Giants' Wall?" asked Cealla.

"It is a house of stone, all broken now, which stands in the woods," said Readda. "A cunningly-made thing. I have not been there since I was a boy."

Cealla kept silent. He had not been able to run the woods when he himself was young. He had lived in the village all his life, and not known there was anything wonderful in the woods.

But the place made him afraid when he saw it. There was a high wall, of smooth stones, suddenly standing up among the trees. The top was ragged, and fallen stones lay all around with grass and sorrel growing over them. Drifts of old-man's-beard and dark ivy clambered over the wall. The gateway in it had a great stone lintel, supported by a pile of white stones made round, and straight like a tree trunk. Cealla shuddered to think of the might of the builders, or else of their magic runes, for surely it was beyond human skill to shape the hard stone so.

But Readda walked straight through, under the tall lintel, and called the others after him. Beyond, there was a courtyard with ruined walls round it. Grass and tall thistle grew in between, and broken stone lay everywhere. In the centre was an upright wand of stripped hazel, with a little cross-piece tied to it, making the shape of a sword stuck point downwards in the ground. In one corner was a blackened ring upon the grass, where a fire had lately been lit.

"Well," said Readda, looking round, "now we know what kind of bear we are looking for." He made the sign of Thor's hammer on his forehead, and then struck down the cross of twigs. "Some go round that way, some this," he said.

Splitting up, the men cautiously worked their way round the ruin.

Cealla and his party were nearly halfway round when cries went up from the other side. They ran to join their fellows. The others were struggling with something caught in one of their nets. The net covered a dark mass, which fought and heaved and took three men to hold down. Cealla's dogs growled, and their hackles rose, but he called them off for fear they should bite one of his friends in the confusion. It was getting dark and difficult to see.

At last some heavy blows with a branch of wood subdued the captured beast, and they slung it, still netted, on a pole to carry home.

"What is it?" whispered Cealla to the next man.

"No bear, that's certain," he replied. "A woodwose, and a fierce one."

It was pitch dark when they got their catch back to the village. To keep it safe for the night they simply drove a stake through the net in which it was tied, deep into the ground. In the red flicker of their torches they could see it struggle in the net to free itself, and they could see that it was caught fast.

"It is a woodwose," they told their wives.

"Give it water, and come away," said Readda.

The fire in Readda's hut had burnt so low that there was nothing in the smooth black darkness except a little glowing patch of scarlet cinders.

"Mother, Mother," whispered Totta in the dark, "what's a woodwose?"

"A forest troll," said his mother. "One of those who had the land before us. Before we came."

Creeping out of their huts in the first light of day the children saw that the bear was really a man. He had black hair, very dark, growing thickly on his arms and on his chest. But they had thought he was a bear because of the great shaggy bearskin cloak he wore around his shoulders. Now he sat squatting, and glared at them through the web of rope which held him.

"Poor thing, poor thing," said Wulfrun softly. "I wish we had not told about him." But when it seemed he heard her, and turned his head to look at her, she became frightened and ran away.

"We must take him to Arnulf," said Readda.

"Arnulf is old now," grumbled Offa. "His words wander. He will talk and talk."

"He is still our lord, and lord of all this valley," insisted Readda. "We must go to him."

A little procession of them formed in the village, not early in the day, for come what might the corn had to be planted, but after midday, when a morning's work had already been done. In the meantime the woodwose had had nothing to eat except a handful of crusts left over from Wulfrun's breakfast. They did not risk undoing the net, but carried him on a rod over their shoulders, laboriously, for Arnulf's hall was in a village higher up the valley, and the captive was not light.

All the men of Arnulf's village came out to look, the women with them, and the children clinging to their mothers' skirts. Arnulf's own thanes stood round, and Arnulf came to his door, and sat upon a chair carried out for him, and the man in the net was set down on the ground before him. Arnulf was very old now. Each time they saw him again it seemed to them he had grown older since the last time. His hair was white, and his beard hung down from his chin past his sword belt, which was not as far as it had once been, for he was bent as though carrying a burden on his shoulders. But in spite of Offa's disrespectful words, there was a glint in the old man's eyes that showed that the hoarfrost on his ancient head had not frozen his wits yet.

"Undo that net!" he said.

Cealla and Readda jumped to obey him. They uncorded the net, and then stood back, well out of the way, for they thought the thing was spiteful. For an instant it made no move, and then it unbowed its head, and shook itself free of encumbrance. Slowly the man stood up, uncoiling his cramped limbs, and stretching, and he stood higher and higher, towering over Cealla and Readda, till they fell right back into the crowd, and were amazed at their luck in having caught him. He was a man of great girth, as well as of great height. His wide shoulders were dressed in a mantle of thick fur, and his hair was long, and so dark that the streaks in it showed like silver, shining on his temples and in his close-cropped beard. He stood up, and he looked straight at Arnulf, and he said nothing at all.

"Ah!" said Arnulf at last. "I never thought to see you again."

The woodwose returned his stare. Then, "No man loses an enemy as easily as that," he said.

"An enemy?" said Arnulf. "I had forgotten that."

"*Forgotten?*" cried the other, raising his voice. "Shall I remind you? Shall I, with all your people listening, remind you what sort of man you are?" He spoke English oddly, on a slightly singing note, like the voice of a slave, but he bore himself all the time more like a king.

"I had forgotten that," said Arnulf, still softly. "No feelings burn me now. I am an old tree and the sap no longer wells up into my heart. Each day I think less of the past, and more of what there will be for supper."

His calm seemed to enrage the woodwose, who clenched his fists till the veins stood out upon the backs of his hands, and ground his heel in the dust as he stood.

"Cast back your mind at least to see how this treatment compares with the welcome I gave you, when I was lord here," he said. "Were you beaten and starved as I have been? Or did I give you meat and drink, and a place by the fire in my house, and gold torques to wear upon your arms?"

"You are right, you are right, Dux," said Arnulf. "My thanes, bring out a stool for this man, and a horn of ale, and a loaf of bread. Anyone coming from so long ago is welcome to me now, friend and enemy alike." And with this a steadier note sounded in Arnulf's quavering voice, and men went running to obey him.

"I should not be welcome were I to remind you further," said the man called Dux, with a kind of grim satisfaction. "I have long turned over in my mind how little you would have to say for yourself, if I stood face to face with you, and accused you!"

A faint tone of amusement crept into Arnulf's voice. "You were right, for as you see, I find little to say to you. But you, Dux, say all you like, if words are what you came for."

But the stool, and the bread, and the ale-horn having now arrived, the Dux sat down, and ate ravenously.

Everyone watched him. Little by little the slaves had put down their work, and come creeping up to stand behind their masters and see and hear with them, so that in Arnulf's kitchen the supper pot was fast boiling dry, and in the field behind

Brunhelm's house a lamb bleated pitiously in the thorn bush that had caught it, and nobody came.

Sitting down, the woodwose did not look so much bigger than other men, and although he still looked uncommonly black, it seemed shameful to Readda to be afraid of something so pitiously hungry; and it occurred to him that he and his neighbours had caught the woodwose, and yet they had not been heard.

He spoke up. "This stranger should take care how he threatens Arnulf, who is lord here," he said. "There is nothing he can tell us that we do not know. We know very well how we came here."

"Do you then?" asked the Dux, speaking between mouthfuls, and turning upon Readda the fierce gaze of his coal-black eyes.

"Oh yes," said Readda. "We have a song about it, that we can all sing."

"Oh yes," said Totta, looking round from behind his father's knee. "It is a good song, very long, and it has Arnulf's name in it, though it is true they sing it in the next valley too, and the way they sing it there, it has nothing about Arnulf at all. . . ." He broke off with a squeak, for his father had clapped a hand over his mouth to stop him, and was shaking him wrathfully.

The stranger's lip curled in visible contempt. But Arnulf was rocking himself to and fro in his chair, his mouth stretched wide in a grin of toothless glee, and laughing a cracked gasping laugh, which quickly made him cough. It took him a long time to get his breath back, and then he said "Come, Dux, would you like to hear the song, since you are in it, though not, like me, by name? I am sure Readda here will have his boy sing it to you!" and he rocked with laughter again.

"A harp, bring out a harp!" cried the delighted onlookers, for songs were usually kept for winter evenings, and the chance of entertainment in the middle of the autumn sowing was rare indeed. The crowd moved closer in. A little wooden harp was brought out, and Readda took it, and struck the notes for Totta to sing.

"Listen! we have heard of the glorious deeds
Of our princes, in days of old!"

the childish voice rang clear.

The tune of the song was the same, line after line, as it was the story in the song men listened for. The story told how there had once been a time when this land belonged to Bretmen. Then a great king rose up in a far country, whose thanes were the bravest in the northern lands, and his fame spread far and wide. The Bretmen sent to him for help, because they were greatly afflicted with strong enemies, and they could not win battles. The king sent out his thanes to help them, and many of the famous warriors went into Bretland. The song gave all their names, and Arnulf's name was among them.

As the words of this song rang in his ears, the proud bearing of the Dux slowly changed. He sat in an attitude of terrible sadness, stone-still. The marks of the years upon his face deepened; they could see that he too was an old man; younger than Arnulf by many years, and yet himself with perhaps three-score years behind him. The holiday feeling that the song had brought to the onlookers faded away as they looked at him.

Totta ran out of breath, and faltered, and the harp was passed to Aelward, a lad of nearly twenty, who was Arnulf's great-grandson. But before he struck the guiding notes upon the strings, the Dux spoke up.

"You have left out the tale of your misfortunes, Arnulf. If the song told all that you owed to me, it would make your treason show in its true light! You have left out the glory and the generosity of my people, so that no memory is left of all that you destroyed!"

"The glory of your folk?" said Arnulf. "That must be one of those things I have forgotten. I remember that they did no work, and had such soft hands that even the hilt of a sword could wound them let alone the blade! I remember that they were so weak-minded they could not remember their own tales, but needed runes upon paper to keep their word-hoards safe. I remember that they lacked strength even to sit upon stools to eat, but lay like sick men, lolling upon couches, wearing white cloaks, and calling themselves citizens, or senators, or some such fooling word, and scorning those who farmed and fought for them!"

The Dux jumped to his feet in anger, and cried out in a strange jumbled tongue that nobody could understand.

"As for the other thing," continued Arnulf evenly, "the tale of my misfortunes before I came to you, why, if you think it would make a better song, take the harp, and put it in!" And now the danger in his mild voice could be heard by everyone, and the chill of it held all the onlookers silent.

The Dux said, "It is not true that you came as a hero whom we asked to come to our aid. You came with scarcely a thread to your back, and with no weapon even at your side, because in your own land there had been a famine, and the people blamed the king for it, and had driven you away. You offered me your skill in battle as payment for the bread you begged from me. And because you were a king, I took pity on you, and gave you lands and a place among my people. And I loved you for your courage, and the grandeur of your ways, and I gave you great gifts, and a ship, and sent you to bring more men like yourself."

"And so I did, I did," said Arnulf, but while he spoke he was laughing again, with a savage, cold mirth. "Will you hear more of the song, that you may add to it?"

"I do not need to hear it," said the Dux bitterly. "I can guess how it will go on." His hearers were disappointed, for the next passage was one they liked, full of battle and blood. "It will say that you fought battles for us, and won them all. That is true enough. And it will say that I promised you land, and then re-fused to give it, which is a lie! I gave and gave, and still you wanted more. I gave land till there was none for my own people, and still you brought one man after another, saying he had fought, or his father had fought my battles and he had no patrimony. You would not be content with any payment, but wanted to inherit all and cast out the true heirs. You wanted to be lords along with us, and bring your barbarous ways into our ancient realm. That is the truth behind your lying song!"

It was clear from the way he looked round him that the Dux expected to be struck down for speaking in this way; but no-body raised a hand against him till Arnulf spoke, and when Arnulf spoke it was still in the same unruffled icy voice.

"No, Dux," said Arnulf, "that is not the truth." And then, with a glitter of triumph in his pale eyes, "But if you want truth you can have it. The truth is that you wanted something for nothing. You thought we could be kept as dogs are kept for hunting, and cast out of sight and sound when the hunt is over. You thought we would remain poor grateful wanderers, year after year, and you did not reckon on the passing of time. Look round you, Dux, and see. The old men here are my sons and their companions, and then there are my sons' sons, and their grandsons. You did not reckon that we would have sons who would grow up here, knowing no other home, feeling their right like your right, and wanting an equal share in the land they fought for. The truth is that there was no land for our sons, and no shrines for our gods, and so when Ælla the great warlord came over the sea to us, we turned on you and drove you out. He became the Bretwalda, and the king of the South Saxons, and since then the ways of this place have been our ways. Is that enough truth for you, or will you have more? The song does not tell that I was a king in exile when I came to you; you complained of that. Now have the truth instead; I was a convicted thief, fleeing from justice. The rusty sword I inherited from my miserable father was good enough for scaring the folk of lonely farmsteads, and carrying off the handful of coins they kept hidden beneath their floors; it was good for nought else, and soon there was a hue and cry after me. . . ." Arnulf spoke loudly, with wicked joy in his voice, watching the Dux all the time, and not seeing the shock on the faces of his own people.

". . . so I fled here," he cried, "and found that any fool tale would be believed, and any man who was brave enough to rob a farm would seem brave enough to lead an army !"

"The wolf that feeds on corpses is not more vile than you !" said the Dux, and he spoke in a hoarse whisper, as though Arnulf's truth had taken his breath away.

"Am I a king, Dux, a hero?" crowed Arnulf. "Then it is you who made me one ! Perhaps you are right, and I do owe you gratitude !"

The old man's ugly cackling laugh rang loudly in the stunned silence. Then the crowd laughed too; laughed wildly from shock, from disillusion, from delight at his impudence and cunning. All round the Dux their voices hooted in harsh derisive mirth. And there was nothing he could do with his anger. He stood and shook with it from head to foot.

"You had better not have come back, Dux," said Readda at last, feeling sorry for him.

The woodwose recovered his dignity at once. "I came to find out what has happened to my people, before I die," he said.

"It is in the song," said Arnulf maliciously. "Sing it to him, Aelward."

But now they had all had enough of the old man's cruel game. "Lord Arnulf . . ." said Aelward, protesting.

"*Sing!*" said Arnulf in a terrible voice.

Trembling, Aelward sang. The people listened uneasily, hearing the tale of bloodshed as though for the first time, for the first time as though the names in it were the names of real men. The song told of the wars of Ælla and of his victory, and of the place of slaughter, and of the great numbers of Bretmen slain. And after the victory the men of the South Saxons killed all the Bretmen, until none were left alive, and drove them out of the land, and took the great kingdom for themselves. There was no mercy shown to the conquered, but all were killed . . .

A little tremor ran round the circle as Aelward reached the terrible line:

"*Because they had been abandoned by their lord.*"

The people held their breath, and all looked at the Dux, for it was true that he was still alive, when a brave man would have been dead.

"That is the truth. Take your answer and go," said Arnulf.

The Dux did not even flinch. "You murdered them all?" he asked.

"All. And laboured many days to bury them," said Arnulf savagely.

"There are none of your people here," said Aelward to the Dux, speaking gently. "We have never heard of a Bretman in all our valley. They are gone without trace."

"Without trace?" cried the Dux. "Look at yourselves!" He turned round to face the crowd which circled him. "Do you not know the Saxons were fair; all of them? They had pale hair, and blue eyes. Look at yourselves!"

And men looked at each other, as though seeing for the first time the brown hair, the green and hazel eyes, the dark locks among the fair, and the blazing red of Readda's kin. And among the slaves, heads were even darker, though there too some were fair.

"You are a mongrel pack!" said the Dux, and then turned to Arnulf again. "*Lord*," he said, framing the word slowly, "you have honours to match your years, and you see your children and your children's children stand up tall before you. When it comes to a struggle between you and me, you out-wit me, as you always did. But now, will you not tell me what happened to my kin, when the great battle was lost for me?"

Then suddenly there was no glee in Arnulf's face, or in his voice. He sounded old and tired. "Your son we flogged and hanged for calling himself a prince," he said. "Your daughter was taken as a bed-slave by Wulfwin, the sword-smith. She had three children, all slaves from the day of their birth. The first died in the year we had a plague of coughing-sickness; the second was hanged to turn away the wrath of Woden, in a year when the harvest was bad. The youngest still lives. He was freed when his master died, and he farms a churl's holding down the valley. If I am not mistaken, he had a hand in catching and beating you."

For a few moments the Dux stood with bowed head, not

moving; and Cealla had time to realize that he himself was the freed-slave of whom Arnulf spoke. He raised a hand to his black hair, bewildered. Arnulf sat blinking the lids of his watery eyes, and his hand lost its grip on the arm of his chair, and wandered, shaking. If he was thinking of anything at all now, it was probably of his supper.

Then the Dux turned round. He looked searchingly at Cealla. All eyes looked with him, and Cealla shrank from them. He was not used to getting much attention.

"Come away with me, grandson, and be a prince, as your royal blood entitles you," said the Dux grandly. "I have a kingdom still to defend, and a caister to defend it from. You shall lead a band of brave warriors, and be called their lord. Will you come?"

Cealla looked down, away from the dark blazing eyes. "I have my corn to plant," he said unhappily. Then, cheering up a little he added, "But it is not the way of our folk to turn their backs on their kin. If you are kin of mine, come home with me, and there shall always be a stool beside the hearth for you, and a ladle from the stew-pot for your bowl."

"The slave-iron bit deep into your heart, that you can make such an offer to me, to a king!" cried the Dux.

"Were you to work in the fields, and hunt in the forest for the food and fire you live by, you would not think so little of them!" cried Cealla, angered, and speaking proudly.

And looking at Cealla's angry face, the Dux smiled, suddenly, a smile that quickly turned into bitter self-mockery. "No," he said. "I will go back to my patch of hill-rock and heather, and my half-dozen tattered men, and be a king there alone. But you are still my heir, entitled to all I have left. Take your inheritance!" And he put into Cealla's hand a small disk of coppery silver.

Cealla looked at it, and found it was a coin. He had never held one before, though he had seen one which Arnulf had, and proudly showed round. The coin had rune-writing round a man's head. MAXIMIAN DUX. Cealla could not read it.

"Thank you," he said, turning the coin over and over. "Perhaps this will bring a better husband for my girl, when the time comes for her to marry."

But the Dux had turned and gone at once, and was striding away up the hillside to the top of the valley.

Running some way behind him went Wulfrun. She must have been hiding somewhere all this time, and she cried after him, "Woodwose, woodwose, they are going to burn down the wood this winter to make a new field, and then where will you go?"

He neither stopped, nor turned his head.

"Oh, woodwose," cried the child's voice, shaking with tears, "there will be no wild for you to hide in, nowhere for you to go!"

But he was already out of sight among the trees. Clutching his penny Cealla started up the hill to fetch his daughter and dry her tears. A slave-woman poured water in the pot to save Arnulf's burnt supper, and someone set free the bleating lamb.

Cædmon

In this monastery of Whitby there lived
a brother whom God's grace made remarkable. . . .
Whenever all those present at a feast took
it in turns to sing and entertain the company,
he would get up from table and go home
directly he saw the harp approaching him.
On one such occasion he had left the house
in which the entertainment was being held
and went out to the stable, where it was
his duty to look after the beasts that night. . . .

*W*ith these words Cuthwin, eighty-four, formerly bailiff of farmlands attached to the monastery at Whitby, spoke to the young monk Bæda at Jarrow, recalling certain memories:

Mother Hild and Brother Cædmon died in the same season. May Lord God guard their souls for ever. That was the year of grace six hundred and eighty, the next but one after the year of the comet. My dear wife, Osthryth, died in that year too.

Abbess Hild . . . Brother Cædmon . . . yes, I knew them. I was there when they first met. Do you know that?

But now? They're names now, that's all. Their bodies are one with the earth, even as if they had never been.

Wait, though! I'm dreaming. What use to you are all these vague words? You've asked me for memories. I must go back, farther back. Brother Bæda, forgive an old man for beginning at the end. Old men think more and more about death, more and more every day. I must go back to the beginning.

Cuthwin half-closed his eyes and passed a hand across his brow, trying to clear the mists from his mind.

Let me think . . . I knew Cædmon as a boy; he was Cutha's son. We played together as children, picked up jet on the strand, came walking once with others to this great wall that Hadrianus built. Look at it! The grey snake that curls from here to Solway in the west. Yes, I've been here before . . . seventy years ago. And not since then. It's a long way from Whitby, a long way for boys to walk. And for old men too.

It was four days' march, I think; two days each way. Coming and going, we slept under the stars. The stones cut our sandals to pieces, gashed our feet like knives. Often we stopped and bathed our feet in the sea; the salt kicked in our wounds. Yes, I remember it well, even after all these years. We marched along, singing, imagining we were legionaries. Singing? Singing, did I say? You may well smile. That, after all, is the point of the thing. That's why I'm here. No. Cædmon didn't sing, *could not* sing. He just marched, and left the singing to us.

Crowthroat Cædmon. That's what we used to call him. Caw. Caw. Old Crowthroat.

I remember how once we forced him to sing. We stood in a circle round him, coaxed him, teased him, bullied him, until . . . caw, caw. We laughed and laughed. How we laughed! Tears streamed down our cheeks.

And down Cædmon's cheeks too . . . you know, Brother Bæda, you know how boys are amongst themselves.

Cuthwin tapped his staff on the ground meaningfully. A harmless beetle scuttled for cover. The old bailiff, eagle-eyed, saw it and crushed it with his staff.

That's how they are! Exactly like that.

. . . Where was I, Brother Bæda? I'm wandering, I know. You must forgive me. This remembering, it's like stumbling through early-morning mist.

Yes, yes. Cædmon. We grew up together, you know. We worked the monastery land together, we sheared sheep together and helped the cows at calving time. I married; Cædmon didn't. That was the only difference. One day was much like another; one season succumbed to the next. The years slipped past. We hardly noticed them.

Then, one spring, old Edmund the bailiff died. He had a sudden stitch. We said prayers, we sang the charm, but it wasn't any good. Fate took him off. That was the next year after Mother Hild had come to the monastery.

Well! Cædmon was three years older than me. Let me think. He would have been forty-four . . . no . . . forty-five at the time. He should have been the next bailiff. But fate goes her own way. Mother Hild appointed me. She made me bailiff in old Edmund's stead.

Cædmon wasn't the kind of man to bear a grudge. Being passed over, I mean. He minded all right. He minded. But he was a gentle man, never a quarreller. He wasn't a leader either; in fact, I'd say he was always the odd-man-out. Still, pleased as I was to be bailiff, I must admit it troubled me a bit at the time.

It was six years later that they held a synod at Whitby. That was the year of grace six hundred and sixty-three, the year before the eclipse and the plague. The synod began in the last week of September. It's what happened then, one night that same week, that I've come here to Jarrow to tell you about.

Cuthwin shifted uncomfortably on the hard trestle bench and paused for a moment, summoning up all his energy. Then he began:

Yes, September it was. The harvest had been gathered in; and it was a good harvest, the best for a number of years if I remember rightly.

We arranged to hold a feast—a kind of thanksgiving. Every-one who worked on the monastery lands was welcome; there were about thirty of us. We held it at the farm, half a mile from the monastery itself.

You look surprised, Brother Bæda. Have you no farm here, attached to the monastery?

Well! We have. We keep pigs there, cattle too. The sheep-pens are near by. You can hear the hungry wolves at night, in winter especially. My scalp tingles when I hear them howl.

I'm dreaming again. Where was I . . .? Yes, the feast. You can imagine it. Meat and fruit and cheese. Mead and ale in plenty. Nothing was wanting.

September's a fine time for a feast. The air's sharp, sometimes there's hoarfrost. It's good to sit by the fire. The day's ache dulls inside you; you drink, you sing, you fall asleep . . . and then again you wake, somehow prepared, somehow ready for the same hard day all over again.

But the feast, yes. Well! We ate our fill. And then, as always, we began to pass round the harp. As bailiff, I sang first. I forget what, now . . . perhaps it doesn't interest you anyhow. May-be it was a riddle. Yes, maybe it was. I like riddling.

Then I handed the harp on. Another man sang. And all the time we were drinking, drinking . . .

Anyhow, this is what happened. Cædmon saw that it would soon be his turn to sing. I remember watching him, watching and wondering what he'd do. He turned white, chalk-white. Well! I'd often seen him do that before. At feast after feast. Just to look at him used to chill me to the marrow. But then do you know what he did? He suddenly rose from his place at the bench and made for the door.

"Hey!" I shouted. "Where are you off to? Where are you going, Cædmon?"

Cædmon gave me a scared look. You know, like a boy caught stealing apples. "It's my turn to guard the cattle tonight," he said. "I'll be in the cattle stall."

That was it; he was gone. Out into the night.

I can't understand it, Brother Bæda, I can't understand it even now. We'd have teased him, of course. We'd all have had a good laugh. But I mean, what does it matter? If he couldn't sing, he *couldn't* sing. Poor old crowthroat. Did it matter all that much to him?

Cuthwin paused. He seemed to look at Brother Bæda. But what he saw, with his mind, was the farm, the merry-making, Cædmon's pale face.

Yes, that was Cædmon. The odd-man-out. Always the lonely one.

Well! We let him go. Perhaps we were too drunk to pull him back. Anyhow, we let him go.

We slept in the farm that night, of course. Some of the men brought in straw and laid it down. We jostled for the best places round the fire. I must admit, I can't remember very much about it. . . .

But the next thing I knew, someone was shaking me by the shoulder, saying "Cuthwin, Cuthwin. Wake up!"

I opened one eye, then the other. You know who it was? Cædmon!

I scrambled to my feet. Oh! My head, my head was hammering. Mead, Brother Bæda. Mead! The devil stirs it with his little finger.

"What's wrong, Cædmon?" I said. "Is everything all right?"

Cædmon smiled at me. I remember that. I remember that smile. "Yes," he said. "Everything's all right."

"Well . . ." I began.

"Follow me," he said. "Dawn's breaking. If we stay in here, we'll wake the others up."

"Wake *them* up?" I said. "No! Not them."

Cædmon led me out. There was pale green and blue in the east. Night was rolling westward. "Well," I said. "What is it? What's wrong?" I can't say I was too pleased at being woken up. And my head! Oh! My head!

"Listen! I'll tell you," Cædmon said in a low, urgent voice. "You must listen carefully."

"I'm listening," I said. You know, Brother Bæda, I was rather startled by his tone. Cædmon was always such a mild man.

Well! This is what Cædmon told me, as sure as I'm called Cuthwin.

"When I left you last night," he said, "I went to the cattle-stall. You remember, it was my turn to stand watch. I found a warm place amongst the straw . . . and there I fell asleep. Forgive me, Cuthwin. I don't know what it was. The mead, maybe. Maybe just the warmth. Anyhow, I fell asleep."

I remember frowning at Cædmon, thinking: What's he telling me this for? What if the wolves . . .? What use is a sleeping man? And yet I didn't interrupt him. There was some-thing about his manner. Anyhow, he went on:

"While I was asleep, I had a dream . . . I think it was a dream. A man came and stood beside me in the stall. I can't describe him. He was tall and fair . . . and half smiling. This man called me by my name. 'Cædmon,' he said. 'Sing me a song.'

"I quivered in my dream. 'I don't know how to sing,' I said. 'That's why I'm here. I left the feast for shame.'

"But this man said to me, 'Nevertheless, you shall sing to me.'

"'What shall I sing?' I asked him. 'What shall I sing about?'

"And the man replied, 'Sing about the creation of all things.' His voice was commanding. I felt compelled to obey. And that's what I did, Cuthwin. I obeyed. To my astonishment, I began to sing.

"I can see what you're thinking, Cuthwin—a dream, just a dream. But listen! When I woke up, I found I could sing. The same song I sang in my dream. Words I'd never heard before, to a strange melody."

Well, Brother Bæda, I was amazed. How *could* it happen to Cædmon, I thought? I'd known Cædmon all my life. Could it really be true?

The next moment, Cædmon had opened his mouth and was singing. There we were, old crowthroat and I, standing under the dawn sky. And this is what he sang:

> Now we must praise the Ruler of Heaven,
> the might of the Lord and His purpose of mind,
> the work of the Glorious Father; for He,
> God Eternal, established each wonder,
> He, Holy Creator, first fashioned the heavens
> as a roof for the children of earth.
> And then our guardian, the Everlasting Lord,
> adorned this middle-earth for men.
> Praise the Almighty King of Heaven.

It was beautiful, Brother Bæda, really beautiful. I'd never heard the like of it before. I almost thought I was dreaming myself. . . . But what was I to do?

"You must take me to the Abbess Hild. That's what you must do," Cædmon said. "You're the bailiff. Take me to her and tell her of this miracle."

So that's what I did, Brother Bæda. As soon as the sun was

up, we walked together to the monastery. The birds sang to speed us on our way; dew lay thick on the grass.

Mother Hild agreed to see us. May God grant her soul peace. She was surrounded by many others . . . I can't remember their names. All those who had come to the synod. King Oswiu himself was there, I know. So was Wilfrid who became Bishop of York. I can't remember the others . . . No . . . Forgive my memory. But I never saw such a company; my knees fairly knocked together.

Anyhow, I told Mother Hild all Cædmon had said. I remember how he stood there, strangely confident. More confident than me. More confident than I'd ever seen him before. You could see he had some inner strength.

Well! When I'd finished my story, they gave me leave to go. I'd got the day's work to attend to.

Cædmon I left with that great company . . . alone. Yes. The odd-man-out. He always was.

And there you are, Brother Bæda! That's really all I can tell you. The rest of the story's not mine to tell.

The young monk Bæda had listened intently to Cuthwin. His eyes were bright and keen, his hands interlocked and motionless. For several minutes, the two of them sat silent, each with his own thoughts. Then Brother Bæda rose, took the bailiff's right arm, and helped him to his feet. He said:

Bailiff Cuthwin, I thank you with my heart for the help you have given me. Brother Cædmon was truly a man whose life, vision and works bear witness to the living God. Be certain, I will weld your words into a common memory.

So saying, Brother Bæda helped Cuthwin across the courtyard to the little room that had been set apart for him within the monastery.

And in that same year Wilfrid, sixty-six, formerly Bishop of all the Northumbrians and friend to Pope Agatho of blessed memory, also spoke to the young monk Bæda at Jarrow, recalling certain memories:

So you want to know about Cædmon? I well recall the time I first saw him—so well it might have happened yesterday.

Isn't it strange, Brother Bæda? One thing the mind remembers; the next it forgets. And there seems to be no sense in it, no principle. Not all we remember really matters; we store up chaff with the grain.

But Cædmon . . . no one would say Cædmon was chaff. I saw him first at the time of the synod. That was the year of grace six hundred and sixty-three. In September it was, I think . . . I wouldn't swear to it.

You've heard about the synod, of course. There was that argument over how to determine the date of Easter. The universal church used one method, the Scots used another. For a long time the two parties just agreed to differ. But the argument increased; there was much bitterness. It threatened to split the church in Northumbria. So at last the two sides decided to meet. . . .

You will know of my views on the subject. I was of the party that followed the Roman tradition, the universal church, as was the Frenchman Agilbert, Bishop of the West Saxons. I wasn't a bishop then, of course. I was still at the monastery of Ripon. It was the year after—my thirty-first year—that Agilbert consecrated me. But I acted as spokesman at the synod, for Agilbert had only French.

Bishop Colman of Lindisfarne was our chief opponent, with Cedd, Bishop of the East Angles, and several Scots priests. I can't remember their names now.

And Hild . . . she was for Colman, you know. I could never understand that; she was so wise in other things. She was a most wonderful woman, Brother Bæda. There'll never be an abbess better-loved than she.

King Oswiu himself acted as arbitrator. And Aldfrith, our King for fifteen years already, he was there too. He was a mere stripling then.

But don't let me bother you with all these names and details. It's Cædmon you want to hear about. It was one morning at the end of the first week of the synod. We had reached a deadlock. It seemed we might altogether fail to come to an agreement. *We* certainly weren't going to give way; and it didn't look as if Bishop Colman was either.

We were all wrangling over some point or other, when suddenly the great hall door swung open: Cædmon stood on the threshold.

Bishop Wilfrid paused, smiling at his recollection. Outside the monastery at Jarrow, the day's light was beginning to fail; the colours in Brother Bæda's room began to fade.

He was a big man—taller than I am. You had the feeling that he didn't know what to do with his limbs. He was awkward, gangling.

He had dark, shaggy eyebrows; and black eyes, black as sloes. They were like wounds, somehow, wounds open for all to see. . . .

There was another man with him that morning. His bailiff, I suppose. I can't remember his name; perhaps I never knew it.

Mother Hild spoke to them kindly, told them to come in. She was a remarkable woman, Brother Bæda. Anyone else would have told them to go away, to come back another time. I would have, certainly. After all, we were deep in discussion. But no! Not Mother Hild. She sensed something had happened —something out of the ordinary.

They came into the hall. The bailiff told us exactly what had happened; you know the story. Indeed, who doesn't? And all the time Cædmon stood silent beside him, looking at us with a steadfast gaze.

As soon as the bailiff—yes! Cuthwin! that was his name—as soon as Cuthwin had told his story, he asked leave to go. Why, I can't remember. Anyhow, he went.

Then Mother Hild turned to Cædmon and asked him, "Will you sing to us now, the same song you sang in your dream?"

And Cædmon began to sing. Brother Bæda, in that song he unlocked his heart. As a man, he was always nervous, always shy. Singing praises to God, he was strong and confident.

But what was he singing? As we listened to his words, there was not one amongst us but realized the significance of the thing. For there was Cædmon, cowherd that he was, standing in front of us, doing something never done before. You know what it was as well as I do. He was marrying the new to the old —singing a Christian song, but in the ancient, heathen way; in the manner of the old, heroic poetry. I could hardly believe my ears. Even now, Brother Bæda, I'm astonished at the thought of it. And yet, as we listened, it all seemed so obviously right. After all, we had adapted heathen temples to Christian purposes; it gave people a sense of continuity. And so, why not do the same with heathen poetry?

We were greatly excited by the significance of Cædmon's song, but—you understand—just a little suspicious of its origin. A cowherd? And one, at that, who had never before been able to sing? It seemed impossible. All things, I know, are possible with God. But it wasn't easy to believe that the cowherd Cædmon had dreamed that song. We decided we must put him to the test.

Mother Hild, I recall, asked Cædmon whether he could read.

"No," Cædmon said, and he sighed deeply. And you know, Brother Bæda, he never did learn to read, not a single word.

So Mother Hild took the Vulgate into her own hands and, translating into English as she went along, slowly read some verses from the Book of Genesis—about the creation of man and the rest of God's creatures. Then she asked Cædmon if he had understood them. He said that he had. Then she told him to go away, to meditate on them, and to turn them—if he could—into poetry. And she asked him to come back the next day.

You can imagine the discussion after Cædmon had gone! The whole synod came to life again. And the more we talked about his vision, the less we saw reason to doubt it. I remember saying I thought it was a sign of God's blessing on our work. And I believe it was too.

Brother Bæda's cell was almost dark now. The two men gathered their cloaks about them. And then, once again, the old man and the young bridged the darkness with words.

Well, Brother Bæda, Cædmon came back the next morning. And, need I tell you, his heart and mind were overflowing with poetry? Once again, he began to sing; and as soon as he sang, the shackles of his shyness slipped from him. He was a poet, praising God.

The miracle! The miracle of it! It made us want to shout and laugh and cry. I shall never forget that day until I die.

Then Mother Hild told Cædmon that his vision was a gift from God. She advised him to abandon the secular life and to become a brother in the monastery.

That's what Cædmon did—and you know his legacy. He was instructed in many events of sacred history. And for seventeen years he made poetry whose equal we have never heard, or are like to hear again. He recounted the whole story of Genesis, and much of the Old Testament. He sang of the Incarnation, Passion and Resurrection of our Lord, and His Ascension into Heaven. Until, at last, his heart and mind still strong, his human frame grew too weak for him. He passed away.

We, on earth, will preserve his poetry; like granite, it will endure the whittling of the years. May God preserve his soul in Heaven.

Bæda my friend, that's the true story of Cædmon. I know of none more remarkable, or more worthy of inclusion in your history.

The young monk Bæda had listened intently to Bishop Wilfrid. His eyes were bright and keen, his hands interlocked and motionless. For several minutes the two of them sat silent, each with his own thoughts. Then Brother Bæda said:

I thank you with my heart for the help you have given me. To you, Father Wilfrid, as to Brother Cædmon, all Christians owe a debt of common gratitude.

Another Penda may come from Mercia, or from the North another swarm of heathen Picts. But they will be turned back; the tide is too strong now. . . .

And yet, only a lifetime ago, no more. . . . It is but seventy-three years since King Edwin was converted to the Christian faith. Only seventy-three years since he was persuaded to embrace it because of its message of hope. In that time, the earth of Northumbria has been so tilled that the seed has taken root which cannot be destroyed.

Bishop Wilfrid, I thank you again for all the help you have given me. And in my history, I shall try to weld your words into a common memory.

Brother Bæda fell silent. The monastery at Jarrow was wrapped in

darkness now. Somewhere in the precincts, a bell was tolling. Then
the sound of monks singing lightened the darkness; and the words they
sang flooded into the cell:

> Now we must praise the Ruler of Heaven,
> the might of the Lord and His purpose of mind,
> the work of the Glorious Father; for He,
> God Eternal, established each wonder,
> He, Holy Creator, first fashioned the heavens
> as a roof for the children of earth.
> And then our Guardian, the Everlasting Lord,
> adorned this middle-earth for men.
> Praise the Almighty King of Heaven.

Asser's Book

At that time I also was summoned by the King and came to the Saxon land from the western and farthest parts of Wales. There I first saw the King in the royal residence called Dean. And when I had been kindly received he asked me to devote myself to his service, and be a member of his court, and to give up for his sake all that I possessed in Wales. And he promised to give me a greater recompense.

*T*ODAY came Asser, a famous scholar from St David's Minster, in the kingdom of Dyfed, answering my most earnest invitation to visit me. He is a little Welshman, short and round, much given to waving his hands as he talks. He arrived at a bad moment, coming to me in the middle of young Odda's first singing of a new song, written for me: a war-song. Young Odda has his pride, and it was a good song, so I made Asser sit down and hear it beside me. Then when the song was done his very first words to me were indignant.

"Look you remember, King," he said, "that God is not pleased only by the winning of battles!"

"I do not forget it, friend," I told him. "It's because I know it well that I gather at my court all the greatest scholars and men of God whose fame reaches me, whenever they can be persuaded to come. Your own great reputation has been here long before you, preparing the warm welcome I extend to you now." This made him calm again. He has the grace to blush at flattery.

And I am indeed glad to see him, for he has made a shining name for learning and piety. Also he has made me laugh. He tells me that he is no courtier, and has never before kept company with rough fighting men like my good thanes, but that this does not trouble him because he can find precedents for it—great scholars have consorted with kings before him. He talks of a Frankish scholar called Einhart, of whom, to my shame, I have never before heard tell, who spent so long with Charlemagne that he was able to write his life; and then he asked me so many questions about my father and mother, that I do believe the man means to make his own bid for immortality by writing a life of me! He has made me laugh; and for that I shall give him the fine cross of gold with niello work and enamel that Cynewulf my goldsmith finished for me this day.

I managed, I think, to keep him from seeing that he amused me, but he has made me remember, asking so much about the past. So here I sit, with Pope Gregory's great book lying open upon my knees, and beside me the word-list for the next pages which John, my mass-priest has made for me, and instead of reading I remember. And all the while the candle burns steadily downwards towards the notch which marks the time at which I must go and pray before I sleep. I have allowed no time of day or night for memories, memories. . . .

We were hunting together, Ethelred my brother and I, not far from this house at Dean. We were hunting deer, riding in sunlight over the hill. I cannot at all remember what quarry we took, or whether we took any at all, but I remember lying in the bracken, on my back, to rest before riding home, with Ethelred beside me, and our horses grazing a little way down the slope. He was the king. Over our heads the clouds moved against a pale blue sky.

"Alfred," he said, "you must tell me what you think I should do."

"You are king, Red," I answered. "And I am the king's brother."

"What kind of answer is that?" he complained. "I was a king's younger brother while three of our brothers reigned, and yet I am now the king. It will be no surprise if soon you are in my place."

"I do not think of it."

"Come, brother, you must have thought of it. You must have considered what you think the king should be. Now the Great Army has come, and there will be trouble. What should I do, do you think? Shall I go to Rome, and pray to avert God's wrath?"

"You jest!" I cried, sitting up suddenly, so that the landscape around us swung abruptly into view. Beyond the slopes of scrub and bracken were the fields of the village, shimmering stripes of new corn, banded with the blue flax-flowers just then breaking bud. I remember seeing the roof of this good house, though it had not then the gilded hart's-horns upon the gables. I put those there later, when the house was newly mine.

"I ask in earnest," said Ethelred beside me, still lying on his back in the grass. "Shall I go to Rome?"

"You have to stay here," I said, fiercely. "A king's first duty is to stay. Is that not why King Edmund is called a saint? It cannot be for his skill in war that the East Angles remember him with love; it must be for staying to be killed. And second only to staying," I went on, "it is a king's duty to lead his people in battle, and to win."

Ethelred looked at the sky, not at me. Clouds floated in his blue eyes. "You are wrong," he said. "A king is not different from other men. A king's first duty is not to his people but to God. And his second duty is nothing to do with battles. It is to foster learning and godliness among his people. Edmund was not victorious; but he has drawn many hearts to God."

"What difference will it make if the people are learned and godly," I asked him, "if they lie slaughtered, and the ravens pick their bones?"

"It makes all the difference how people have lived, whenever they die. Do you not know that? You make a king in a Christian land nothing more than a pagan war-lord!"

"He should be much more, of course, I know that," I said. "But he should be a good war-lord first."

"The best war-lord in the world will not win without God's help," said Ethelred. "God first."

"Ah well, perhaps you are right," I said at last. "But do not go to Rome."

"No," he said. "I trust God can hear my voice from where I am." Then suddenly he rolled over, and sat up, and pulled up a handful of grass to throw at me. "But you, Alfred," he cried, grinning, and pelting me with grass, "you growling manger-hound! Haven't you been to Rome yourself, more than once? Easy to bid others stay at home! Do you say battles come before books indeed? And wasn't it you who won the book from our mother by learning to read it first!"

And I stood laughing, fending off showers of grass with my hands. "I'm trying to *fight* you!" he said, jumping round me furiously. "Throw some back, damn you!"

"Brother," I said, choking on my laughter, "how can I raise my hand against my king?"

"Oh!" he cried, outraged, and flung himself at my knees so that we tumbled down together, and rolled down the slope through the bracken, over and over, and came to a stop, gasping, and then we heard voices: the thanes of the court coming to look for us. Hastily we stood up and brushed the bracken off each other, and so they found us looking dignified enough for our positions in the state—except for our shining eyes.

I think that was the last time we were boys together. Trouble closed over us quickly after that. The next summer the sons of Ragnar came, with the Great Army of the Danes, and they did terrible things wherever they went.

There was a great coming and going from the court, and men gathered in every house, and camped in the fields by Winchester. Fear was everywhere, as though it were an odour on the air we breathed. My brother breathed it too.

He called me to his chamber to speak with him alone one night. I remember that we sat with the light of one taper only, and it cast dark shadows on his face.

"They are on the move," he said. "We shall soon be strapping on our war-gear."

"I am ready," I said.

"Brother, you did not claim your share of our inheritance from me; you trusted me with all."

"That I learned from you," I answered. "You did not claim your share when Ethelbert was king. We know it is best to keep the land undivided."

"And I promised to hand all over to you," he said, "when my turn came to die. But in a week either or both of us may be dead. And what will become of our children? They will need lands. If all that we have is to stay in the hands of the king, my sons or yours may be left in poverty."

"Whichever of us lives longer shall provide for the other's children," I said. "We will swear this to each other."

"I hoped you would say that," he said, smiling.

"Surely we would have done so, even without an oath," I said.

But he called the council of all the kingdom, and we swore it before them all. And the armies gathered from far and wide.

The Danes had never before been defeated on English soil, and it was deep winter when they moved into Reading, and made a camp, and mounted attacks on the land of Wessex from there. Yet the Alderman of Berkshire put a band of them to flight with only his own few men beside him, and a few days later Ethelred and I drove them from the battlefield, and chased them all the way to their earth walls at Reading, and then they turned on us and beat us back from their camp. That day my brother and I fought like a single man; it was at Ashdown that the difference between us was shown.

They came in full force along the ridge of hills called Ashdown, plundering the villages in the valleys on either side. It was January, and the corn they took, and the oxen, put the spring sowing in peril. Ethelred marched from Winchester with the armies of every part of the kingdom, and all his thanes, meeting their full force with ours.

At night they camped in the open, and when we came up to the foot of the hills near Uffington we could see their camp-fires glimmering in the dusk, a coronet of fiery sparks for Ashdown. Our own fires were extinguished long before daybreak, and we marched up the hill to meet them. Behind each thane, five and six abreast the men filed up the hillside; in the near-dark. The soft grass muffled footfalls, but the dawn hush was full of the chink and tinkle of buckles and harness, one against the other, and the silken watery rustle of chain-mail byrnies, and now and then the clang of a bumped shield.

What I saw then shines in my mind's eye like something seen only yesterday. The dawn came up over the woods away on our right, and along the skyline at the brow of the hill there was a sheen like light on cold water. Then we saw it was light on steel: on chain-mail, on helmets, ice-bright on the points of spears. At the top of the hill they were waiting for us.

We halted. I looked around for Ethelred. His men were there, yet he was not.

"The king is in his tent, hearing Mass," said Osgar the thane. "He is coming soon."

"Let us make ready," I said. "Call all the thanes to me."

When they had come I once again looked down to see if Ethelred was on his way. Not seeing him, we talked together. The Danes were drawn up in two divisions. Wulfwin said the raven banner of Ragnar's sons flew over one group, and the banners of their jarls over the other. We agreed to make two divisions ourselves, and the thanes rode away to give orders to their men.

Then we were drawn up in battle-ranks, ready. The two shield-walls were made, shields overlapping, locked in line. A cold wind was blowing with the dawn, and the greyness was fading from the light; we could see them watching us, and their banners strained and flapped over their heads. The advantage of the slope was with them, for we faced uphill. There was, I remember, a single stunted thorn-tree on the hillside, crouching, crippled by the winds.

I said to Osgar, "Go and get the king!" Even as I spoke the silence was broken, they began to shout and stamp, and beat the ground with the butts of their spears.

Osgar went, and returned.

"The king answers that he will come when the Mass is finished," he said.

They advanced down the slope a little way. Then they sent arrows hissing towards us. Behind the shield-wall, among the closely-standing men, the arrows found their marks. Louder and louder rang their war-cries in our ears, and from our ranks a sighing, a sound like wind in the grass, as the arrows came again. Anxiously, all men looked at me. I sent Wulfwin galloping headlong downhill to the king's tent, and while he went I watched the Vikings. They were moving. Gently, little by little, the wings of their lines were edging forwards, curving down-hill towards us. Then they came thicker, faster. In a few minutes they would have outflanked us.

Then Wulfwin was beside me, out of breath, leaning down from the saddle, gasping, "The king says he will not leave the service of God for the service of men!"

"Go!" I called to the thanes around me, "Make the shield-walls swing outwards to face those Vikings who are moving down on either side."

"My lord," said Wulfwin, "that will leave the centre defenceless!"

"Do it!" I cried, furious. "The kingdom before my brother," I muttered to myself, clutching my sword and spear.

My own men were around me, waiting. Slowly, as the front ranks wheeled to face the outflanking Danes on either side, a gap opened up in the middle. I waited, waited. The muscles of my face were twitching, my sword-hilt was slippery with the sweat of my hands. Then I screamed, screamed like a maniac, and charged through the opening gap, uphill towards the enemy, with my men rushing and yelling beside me. Brihthelm let loose the banner over my head, I heard it flapping and crack-ing on the tugging wind; the dragon of Wessex spread his red wings above me.

I remember the jarring shock through my limbs as I came to a halt, spread-eagled on the shield of a snarling Dane, with my spear running ahead of me, thrust right through his side. There was a din so loud that my ears thrummed in my head. We shouted, *Wessex, Wessex, Wessex!* I remember losing my foot-ing, and stumbling under a great swinging Danish axe, seeing the blade slicing downwards towards me, above all the noise hearing the whistle as it cut the air. Then my brother was suddenly beside me, and the axe fell harmlessly at my feet, the hand still clenched on the haft of it, severed at the wrist.

"Late, Red, late!" I cried to him.

"And in good time!" he called.

Then we were laughing, laughing, and they were giving ground, backing away from us. We yelled and shoved, and cut them down, and they fell back and back, and then they were running, desperately running, with the brave men of Wessex thundering after them, howling in triumph.

Later I remember riding with Ethelred, with many thanes, across the green back of Ashdown. And all along the miles of grassy hillside the land was strewn with their dead.

We had a victory feast for Ashdown. From all the king's farms in the kingdom there rolled in barrels of ale, carts loaded with chickens and sides of beef and the clay jars which hold the pale sweet mead. Ethelred and I climbed down into the cellars of the palace at Winchester, and opened the treasure-chests, looking for gold and silver to give our thanes a gracious keepsake. We piled up torques, and rings, and armlets, and new cloaks, and drinking-horns, rimmed with wrought silver.

"That is enough," said Ethelred at last, "except for one last man. You, Alfred. What will you have?"

"Pope Gregory's book, that our father brought back from Rome," I said at once.

"But it is in Latin, and you cannot read it!" he cried.

"Still, brother, it is what I want. Let me have it."

"Willingly," he said. "But remember, before you open it, that battles come first with you!" So he mocked me, but he gave me the book.

When I think of him, I like best to think of him at that feast. He was splendidly robed in scarlet, sitting in the high seat, the place of the kings, calling his thanes to him one by one, handing out words of praise, and gifts of plated gold. We were packed so close, side by side upon the mead-benches, that we could hardly move, yet no one went short of drink! From the corner of the hall the minstrel sang all night; first of the deeds of Cerdic, then of the death of Cynewulf, then of the victory on Ashdown. In the middle of the victory song, Ethelred stood up, and stopped the minstrel in mid-line.

"Give the praise to my brother more than to me," he said. "It was his battle."

The song began again, this time with my name in it, coming again and again. But I did not want my brother's glory; I sat, head down, scowling into my ale, discomforted. Then Odda got up.

"I know a better way to sing it," he said, and took the harp. He had a lovely voice, high and strong, and he sang in praise of the love between brothers, that made Ethelred and me trust each other, and stand side by side to meet our enemies, and the enemies of our land.

And so the great battle had its victory song, and it was sung in a way that pleased us both. Because of that song I have given Odda many gifts, many chances to raise his beautiful voice in my halls. I have heard many words from him, and made him prosper. And now I will cherish his son, young Odda, dear to me for his father's sake. I have a long memory now; but there is nothing better to remember than that feast—when all our good friends and warriors were gathered in the warm hall, and the mead flowed freely, and there was laughter and singing, and the night-winds howled harmlessly outside.

How long ago it seems! I thought in my heart that fate had sided with me in the argument, and proved on Ashdown that fighting came first of all; Ethelred thought he had been given victory in reward for his faithful prayer. I was young, and I did not then know that there can be no final victory against the Danes, though there could be final defeat. Long years of war have taught me that.

A few short months after Ashdown, I sat in my brother's place, and put his crown on my brow, myself the king, promoted by death. I did not forget his children. I have not forgotten his saying, that whenever a man may die, it is how he lived that makes the difference. There has been no peace in the land. One Viking band is no sooner defeated than another one comes. When first I was king, I thought of nothing but war. I rode from one end of the land to another, building forts, making new rules for the armies. There have been many disasters and defeats from which it seemed no victory could come. Most of the fine thanes of that far-off time on Ashdown are dead now, like my brother. It is their younger brothers, their younger cousins, their sons who serve me now. And yet we have not been overwhelmed. We have defended the land.

Nevertheless, if I wait for an end to the fighting before I turn to other things, I shall wait till I die. So I think now that a king must do everything at once, be all things at once. That is why I sit here, deep in the night, working at Pope Gregory's book. I mean to turn it into English, and afterwards other books, whichever it is most needful that men should know, so that my people may once more be as learned and godly as they were before the Danes first came.

It is time I am short of; my candles mark its passing, so that I may carefully divide it. And each day I give time to prayer, time to governing, and time to my books. Tonight the flame has melted the notch away, long since, and I am late to my prayers.

But late though I am, I see a light burning in Asser's room, across the yard from mine. I can see it flickering through the wattle shutter at his window. He will be writing, writing the things I told him today—these memories, these memories. I shall soon find him other things to do, other books to work on. He shall translate for me. Work hard tonight, Asser, my friend; you shall soon have no time to finish books of your own!

Leof's Leavetaking

Leaves are green for a little while;
then they fade to yellow, fall
to earth and wither, and become dust.

LEOF had been discarded; no other word would do. Old Leof the poet, poet at Rendlesham to the court of kings. His job was gone, his security was gone, his lord and audience, his bed, his food, his peace of mind. And all for the sake of another, another who was young enough to be his son.

He took little with him the morning he left: the little he owned—the clothes he walked in, this and that in his beaver-skin bag, above all his six-stringer, the harp slung over his back; and he took the great song-hoard stored within his head.

That October morning, there was travelling weather: sun in the bowl of pale blue, bite in the early air. Leof set off southwards, heading for the ferry, heading for Ipswich before sundown.

Away from the hall, between the outbuildings, out of the enclosure he walked, and across the scythed sloping meadow down to the banks of the river. Any man but he would have rejoiced there that day, gazed into the water and let his thoughts float seaward; but Leof saw only the darkness beneath the gleaming mirror, and heard the wild sorrow of the seabirds. He

49

mouthed the words, the exile's words he knew so well, and now, lordless, must live out:

> The cry of the gannet is all my gladness,
> the call of the curlew, not the laughter of men,
> the mewing gull, not the sweetness of mead.

Leof turned his back on the river and lifted his eyes to Rendlesham. Rendlesham, court of the Wuffings. Rendlesham, fit for kings. The great hall towered over the outbuildings, the line of the roof very clear in the cutting air, the antlers adorning the gables singled out by the sun. Leof stood looking at it, stared at it like a man who has returned alive from war to find his wife and his sons and daughters dead. He looked first with his eyes, then only with his heart and mind; and he fell into a waking dream, remembering other days, a time gone now even as if it had never been.

"For I," said Leof, "would never have been an exile as I am now if Offa were still king. He knew my boast was not an idle one: that I could tell lays long forgotten by other men, and that I in the hall could cast a spell on his warriors even as he could spell-bind them before battle. He spoke; I sang; we both knew the power of words.

"Offa respected me. He gave me gifts of gold, and promised me peaceful years if I should grow too old to sing. He knew the time must come when his own face would grow pale, and when old age would shake his hand. He would not have turned me out, to fend for myself and find a new lord."

Leof's lion-face furrowed against the sun, still high in the east over Rendlesham. The wind tangled with his silver mane. His whole form was noble—an outward sign, some people said, of his inward gift. And yet it belied his frailty: the right arm all but useless since he had broken it and it was set crooked; the rheum in his whole bone-house; but worst of all, the painful polyp on his tongue that hurt whenever he spoke. Time and again he had rehearsed the old charm: *Become as small as a grain of linseed, and far smaller than a hand-worm's hip-bone and so very small that you are at last nothing at all.* But the polyp remained.

"He would not have turned me out," repeated Leof, speaking to himself as poets and old men do. "No, not Offa. Leof, he called me; the valued one, the loved one. And I returned his love. But then Kineswitha, his own bride-to-be, was called by God to become a nun; and she persuaded Offa, Offa the king himself, to take holy vows and to renounce his throne." The old poet paused, then grimly smiled, and added, "Loving each other, they married Christ, and so sleep alone.

"And I," he went on angrily, "I am thrown to the four winds by Offa's cousin, Selred the king. And not because my powers are failing, my memory faltering, not at all because of me; only because he has it in his head to further some piffler, some poetaster: his sister's son. Some poet-in-arms, some un-armed-poet, what is his name? Edric. Yes, Edric. Edric of Colchester."

But for all his taunts and his anger, Leof was resigned to his lot. He knew as well as any how every man is bound to further his own sister's son; and he knew in his heart that he was in the hands of fate, the fate God shaped for him.

Resigned, but not impervious. He looked for a last time at the gleaming citadel that had always been his home. Then he closed his eyes to the pain and shivered under the sun. And he turned on his heel, away from Rendlesham.

For an hour, and another hour, Leof walked, fearful of the journey. And he saw nothing but the stones on his path. Leof of all men, the poet who went in awe of nature's mysteries, went now like a blind man, often stumbling, with a stick for friend.

He took the track that followed the course of the River Deben. At first the ribbon of shining water writhed, writhed and sidled, uncertain where to go, and then at last it opened out and straightened, and flew directly to the sea. At the river's neck, just before the estuary, there was a ferry, the water-link with Ipswich and with Colchester, with the kingdoms of the Middle-Saxons and the West-Saxons. Here Leof came.

The sun rose slowly in its low-slung arc; two hours remained before noon.

"Always an hour before noon and always an hour before sundown. Always then, fair weather or foul, and only then," said the gat-toothed ferryman to Leof. And that was that.

There was a swelling in the land at this place, a sandy hoe swept by sharp air, commanding wide views over earth and water. Here the Wuffings burned and buried their dead; it was called the Cemetery of Kings.

Stirred by memory, Leof resolved to set eyes on it once more. He stumbled up the incline, and reached the top of the escarpment, panting. And there he looked about him—looked at the sight he never thought to see again: the eleven great barrows of the Wuffing kings. Some the years had stitched with grass; the rest were still threadbare.

"Ten kings," muttered Leof, "ten kings under the earth. And one barrow for the body lost in battle, for our king borne off by the River Winwaed.

"And I knew five," said Leof, "I sang for Anna, I sang for Æthelhere and his brother Æthewald, sang for Ehe and for Tyttla—as also I knew and sang for Offa, and for Selred the king who has thrown me out."

Leof sat down, overcome with memories: feasting in the hall; courtly ceremonial; warriors shouting, flushed with wine;

his youth, the youth of kings; the relentless passage of time. "Gone," he said. "Gone. Remembered only in men's minds, in my songs. Who knows as much, half as much as I about the Wuffings, their origins and lineage, and all their accomplishment?"

He needed no one to answer him; he knew all questions contain their own answers. "Gone," he repeated. "Gone. They sleep until Domesday. And great gold-hoards lie beside them, gleaming metal given back to the earth, as useless to men as it was before."

"Hoar-oyee! Hoar-oyee!"

Leof started, and scrambled to his feet. He felt dazed by the sun, by the turmoil within him.

"Hoar-oyee!" The ferryman was shouting and waving his arms.

Leof stumbled down the slope, swore at himself for letting the past crowd out his present business; his heart beat fiercely.

"All for one," said the ferryman, pushing the boat out, surly at his lack of custom.

"One for one," said Leof. "That's fair enough."

"One for all," the ferryman replied, "is best for the pocket," and he grinned his gat-toothed grin.

"Until they throw you overboard," Leof said moodily.

The ferryman looked at him, scowled, and decided to leave him alone.

But Leof's mood changed as the ferryman began to punt out into deep water. The wind driving up the course of the river caught at his throat; he threw back his head and filled his lungs with air; the sun flared in the sky; the seabirds shrieked, swooped and rose again with twisting silver in their beaks; he felt strangely comfortable, sitting on the salt-bleached boards, trailing the fingertips of his left hand in the cold water. And he sensed in his mind, or did he even feel, the rippling stream passing under him. "It is so long," he said, "since I was on water."

"Aha!" the ferryman said.

Leof knew, for that moment, the true exhilaration of the traveller at one with the world about him; and for that moment the certainty of his exile, the uncertainty of all else, mattered not at all. The minute was the thing: man and boat and water in harmony. The old man sighed deeply.

Then the short journey was at its end. Leof stood up, the ferryman gave him a hand ashore. The poet thanked him and recklessly gave him a whole *sceatta*. Then the ferryman thanked him profusely, wished him a good journey, said how much he looked forward to ferrying him back next day.

"No," said Leof, "I shall not be coming back this way."

Not one passenger was waiting to be ferried across to the eastern bank of the river, so without further ado the ferryman pushed off once more. Leof watched him go: a blunt man skilled in his ways.

Then the old poet felt weary in his legs for the first time—it was as if the momentary excitement of the water-crossing had drained him rather than endowed him with new energy. So he sat down and decided to eat on the river-bank the food he had brought with him: bread, a large onion, and meat that had been roasted only the evening before. "Soon," he said, "it will be winter: salted meat. Enjoy this, and all things, while you can." And he did, ending his meal by half-emptying his gourd of ale.

"The next meal," he said, "will have to be bought with *sceattas* or with songs. A meal in some hall I have never seen before, mead-drinking with strange faces; warriors who, maybe, will not even know my name. This is the lot of the wanderer, the lonesome man. And yet, some men live through sorrow and learn joy again; like the Phoenix, they rise reborn from their own ashes. If their griefs have passed away, so mine, mine also may."

Leof stood up once more and faced the great pine-forest that divided him from Ipswich. "It is less than three hours walk from here. I shall sleep at Ipswich, and look for a lord there, a friendly lord who will always protect me in return for songs; and if not there, then in Colchester, or in London, or in the land of the West-Saxons my days as an exile may come to an end."

Then he took the track away from the water, and plunged into the forest. The way was soft with pine-needles—each sharp in itself, but together a padding that gave under Leof's tread. Here and there the sun saw an opening, and struck through with a golden knife; for the rest, there was only gloom, a palette of dark brown and dark green, receding here to misty blue, and there to impenetrable grey.

For a little while he walked, and then he saw approaching through the forest-gloom a young man, singing. Leof stopped in his tracks, to look and to listen. And just for an instant he had the feeling that he was looking at himself, young again: the long fair hair; the eager step; above all, the clear resonant voice, singing of spring and summertime while the leaves fell:

> Winter will melt, fair weather will return,
> summer, the scorching sun. The waters
> are restless then. Dear is the welcome one
> to the Frisian wife when the ship sails in;
> his boat is berthed, her own husband is back,
> the man who maintains her, and she leads him home.

Fair weather . . . the welcome one . . . home . . . the words stabbed at Leof now.

As soon as the young man caught sight of him, he broke off his song. "Greetings!" he called. "Greetings!"

"Greetings!" said Leof.

"Am I on the right way for the ferry?"

"You are," Leof said, "but too late for the forenoon crossing, and far too early for the second crossing an hour before sundown."

"I'd swim," said the young man warmly, "if it were not for this harp."

"Harp?" said Leof curiously.

"Look!" said the young man, producing the instrument from behind his back with an air of triumph—as well he might: it was worked with great skill, inlaid with ivory and gold.

"Are you a poet?" asked Leof.

"I am," said the young man.

"We are both poets then," Leof proclaimed joyfully, brandishing his own harp, "both poets under heaven. When poets meet, they should sing."

The young man nodded his head. "We *will* sing," he said. "There was a clearing with water only a little way back, where the sun will warm us and the small stream cool us. Let us go there."

So they went. "I am no longer young," Leof said. "And I have a polyp on my tongue. I am no longer the poet I was. . . ."

"The poet I have yet to become," the young man interrupted gracefully.

So they came to the clearing, which was just as the young man had described. There they sat down, facing each other.

"Youth precedes age; and the young must respect the wishes of the old," observed Leof.

"So. . . ." said the young poet.

". . . you must sing first," concluded Leof, smiling.

Then the young man did not hesitate. He cradled his harp as a woman does her baby and, letting the strings ripple under his fingers in a broken chord, he began to sing.

And all that he sang was well known to Leof, words from the song-hoard of the East-Saxons. The old poet listened, not so much with his mind only as with his whole being. He listened to lays about men who fought and conquered others; men who had won the greatest victory of all, conquering death itself, by living in the memories of other men.

The young poet's limitations were as apparent to Leof as his skills. From time to time he hesitated to find the right word, and from time to time he broke the alliterative pattern; and he relied too readily on phrases that were every poet's stock-in-trade. Yet, for all that, Leof liked his energy, and his style, and his resonant voice. He concluded that the young man's memory was good, his manner impressive, but that he lacked—lacked, as yet maybe—any true singularity.

The song came to an end. The young poet, flushed, looked eagerly at Leof.

"Drink!" said the old man imperiously, handing him the gourd.

"I'll drink from the stream," said the young man.

Leof smiled. "You can sing," he said. "You are a poet."

The young man looked pleased, and inclined his head. He started to say something . . . and then he decided not to.

"Such a song is fit for a king," said Leof loftily; then bitterly, "if such king is fit for the song."

The irony was lost on the young poet who presently, pleasantly said, "And now it is your turn."

"I will sing," said Leof, his voice trembling, rising, as if he was about to sing in defiance of the whole world rather than in response to a polite invitation.

The pines nodded their heads, and the long silver arm of the stream reached into the gloom.

"I will sing," said Leof again, and his voice was urgent, like a race against time. "*Hwæt!*" he shouted. "Listen! Listen!"

Then he began to intone words in a low voice, the murmuring of bees in summer. And he started to sway to and fro. His eyes were closed. He was looking inward only, intent on becoming one with the song, on becoming the song.

The young poet listened, watched, hypnotized. He heard Leof sing of the aged Phoenix, the Phoenix of Arabia:

> When the wind is asleep and the weather set fair
> and the flawless jewel of heaven glows in its holiness,
> when the clouds have dispersed and the mighty deeps
> lie calm, when all storms are spent
> under heaven and when the warm candle of the sky
> gleams from the south, giving light to men,
> then the Phoenix begins to build in the branches,
> to fashion its nest. For its mind is filled
> with a fervent desire to exchange
> old age for youth, to renew its life.

Leof opened his eyes, fierce burning eyes. He rocked to and fro, and told how the Phoenix built its nest of flowers, and how the sweltering sun set light to the bird in its nest:

> Fire engulfs
> the nest of the sad Phoenix; fast and furious
> the yellow flames flicker and the age-old bird is burnt.

The falling yellow sun lanced through the darkness of the branches, washing Leof the poet in gold; it was as if the burning planet itself had heard Leof's call.

And it seemed to the young poet at that time as if the stream stopped, and the stones stepped out of the earthbed to listen; as if the trees stood to listen; as if Leof himself was no mere man of this middle-earth.

As for Leof himself, all he knew was that words came for him and he could use them; and that at all times there were always a thousand turnings and that this time he chose the right ones; this time above all times. And he knew that he had for that moment, that moment, a power over himself—or was it that some power moved him?—and therefore over all things. And he knew that nothing mattered but that moment, which nothing before or after could alter; he knew that nothing mattered but the life of the song which was beyond time, and beyond death. He sang, sang, he sang:

> the house of the brave bird
> is consumed by fire; its corpse grows cold,
> its body breaks apart; the flames die away.
> And afterwards, in the ashes of the pyre,
> is an apple's likeness to be found,
> from which grows a worm, wondrously fair—
> as if it had issued from an egg,
> had broken, shining, out of the shell. In the shadow
> it grows: first it is like an eaglet,
> a fair fledgling; but it increases further,
> in great joy, until it is like
> an eagle come to maturity; and after that
> it is as it was in the beginning, beautifully adorned
> with brilliant plumage. . . .

So the song ended, with that beginning; and the old man, just a man, looked a little older.

But the young poet leaped to his feet, and shouted, and threw his arms about Leof. His cheeks were damp; he wept tears down, unashamed.

Leof was much affected, and returned the young poet's embrace.

"Master," said the young poet.

Then Leof drank ale from the gourd, to loosen his throat and to ease the pain of the polyp on his tongue. He wiped his brow, he looked at the sky. "It is late," he said, "already, and so soon." And then at once, and with greater strength, the full force and misery of his exile redawned within him. "We must hurry," he said, "or you will miss the ferry, and I will not reach Ipswich."

"I will find you," said the young man. "Where will I find you?"

"In yourself," said Leof, and he smiled enigmatically.

"I will find you," said the young man urgently, "for you have the treasure I have glimpsed and cannot hold."

"Go now," said Leof gently, "as I must go. Find the ferry. Tell me one thing only."

"Yes," said the young poet eagerly.

"Your name."

"All this time," laughed the young man, "and we haven't exchanged names. My name is Edric."

Leof stiffened. His body became as rigid as a spear. A shiver played up and down his spine. "What?" he said, "what name?"

"Edric."

"Edric of Colchester?"

"The same," said the young man, delighted that Leof should have heard of him.

Leof was seized with a terrible trembling. He knew, yet he had to make sure. "The Edric who is Offa's sister's son?"

"Yes," said Edric, flattered. "Poet to the court of the Wuffings."

Leof said nothing; he knew only he must say not a thing, nothing. How could he say anything? And what was there for him to say? He stood there, silent, and saw his liferoad behind and before him, his bitter destiny.

"And you?" asked Edric, noticing nothing. "Before we part, tell me your name."

"I?" said Leof. And he passed the back of his good hand across his forehead.

Edric looked puzzled. "Your name," he repeated.

"I," said Leof, "a poet amongst poets, a singer under the skies."

"But give me your name."

"What's in a name?" cried Leof angrily. "A name is for those who belong. I have no belonging."

Edric stared at him, dismayed.

"Fate goes ever as it must," said Leof in a voice suddenly tired, resigned.

"But you . . ." began Edric.

"Go now," said Leof. "Go, go now. Commend me to your king. Fate goes ever as it must."

Then Leof turned away, and moved into the clutching forest. Edric stood looking after him, until he could no longer distinguish him from the trees; then he turned too, and headed for the ferry.

Timeless the song, but time had moved on. It was already near to dusk, the blue hour. Leof walked for an hour, as quickly as his old legs could take him. He concentrated fiercely on the path, attempted to think of nothing, nothing but the way ahead.

He hurried, hurried, tripping often on the knuckled roots. He was an ache; every bone in his body ached; his head and his heart ached and ached.

Pine-trees gave way to oak and beech. Then Leof knew that there was not so far to go. But quickly the light failed, and still Leof was not out of the forest, on the way across the easy meadows to Ipswich.

Then he was lost. It happened as it had to happen. One moment he was on the path, then it was lost to him.

And darkness fell.

For a little while Leof groped. But it was useless; he knew it was useless. He had heard tell that, when there is no light, men who try to walk straight walk only in circles.

Then the old man sat down, dazed, too exhausted now even to think, too exhausted to feel hunger for the food he lacked, aware only of the cold night to come. When he closed his eyes he saw strange lights; when he opened them there was only the darkness.

So he placed his harp beside him, tenderly. Then he gathered his cloak about him as tightly as he could and, shivering a little, he lay back, using his beaver-skin bag for a pillow.

He slept.

And later, much later, sometime before dawn, the shuffling shoaling autumn leaves covered him with a mound.

The Horseman

Then Dunnere spoke and shook his spear;
a lowly churl, he cried out loud
and asked every man to avenge Byrhtnoth's death:
"Whoever intends to avenge our prince
must not flinch, nor care for his own life."

"WHO are you?" demanded the girl Gode.

She had seen him a long way off. Her eagle eye, open for her absent father, singled him out against the dark backdrop of the distant wood. She watched him turn off the sandy road to Colchester and gallop across the acres of scrub, a lonesome figure in a desolate scape.

As soon as she was certain that the rider had left the highway on purpose, and realized he was heading directly for their farm, she called out "Edgar." Her voice was a bell, appealing. And quickly enough her brother, four years old, less than half her age, trotted out of the hut and into the yard, grinning like a little devil. "Demon!" he yelled, "dee-mon!", hoping to provoke her into a small fight.

"Look!" said Gode, pointing, anxious.

And Edgar looked, but in the wrong direction.

Then she took her brother's grubby hand and, stepping back instinctively, they stood together at the entrance to the hut, waiting for the horseman to arrive.

For a moment he seemed to dip out of sight. After that, there was thunder as he spurred his horse up the incline, and into the yard itself. Hens dispersed, squawking.

The rider reined-in his great sweating bay; it pawed the ground, and its hooves kicked up little puffs of dust. A helmet hung at the man's side, and he held a spear of ashwood in one hand. He was wearing a mailcoat that musically clinked and chinked and gleamed under the grey sky.

"Who are you?" Gode demanded again. But this time her voice quavered.

The man ignored her question. Gasping for breath, he ran a hand through his tangled fair hair. Then he looked over his right shoulder, and for a full minute scanned the lonely plain; apparently satisfied, he glanced about him. "Is there anyone in there?" he asked, staring right through them.

Gode gripped Edgar's hand more fiercely.

"Is there anyone in there?" the warrior rasped. "Where's your father?"

"Are you . . ." Gode began uncertainly.

"I'm as English as you are," said the warrior.

"My father's with Byrhtnoth. He's gone to fight the Danes at Maldon."

The horseman said nothing; there was an uneasy silence. "And your mother?" he asked at length.

Gode dropped her head. "She's dead," she said in a steady expressionless voice. And it was as if with that question the horseman had driven his spear-point to her heart. "Dead," she said again, and fiercely, "The Danes killed her."

Then the horseman dismounted.

Gode and Edgar drew back. "I'm not afraid," said Gode.

"You've nothing to be afraid of," said the warrior, and he put his helmet and spear on the ground as if to prove it.

"What do you want?" asked Gode, confused. "Who are you?"

"Godric," said the man, "and what I want is food. Can you give me that?" He smiled at them encouragingly. "Food, and some bandage for a hurt."

"Where have you come from?" Gode asked him.

"London," said Godric, "with a message from the king, from Ethelred himself to the people of Bradwell and Dengie." And guessing her next question, he went on: "Yes, I came by Maldon. No men were fighting there. No Saxons, no Danes." He shrugged his shoulders.

"But didn't—" began Gode.

Godric interrupted her. "Otherwise, how would I be here? I'd be with them, fighting with your father and with Byrhtnoth at Maldon."

Gode felt troubled in her heart and in her mind. It showed in her eyes. "How can it be?" she said. "My father told me. . . . I don't understand. He said the whole fyrd was to gather at Maldon."

Godric shrugged his shoulders again. "I've told you," he said.

"Haven't you heard," Gode insisted, "that Olaf Tryggvason himself leads a great force of Vikings?"

Godric eyed her. "I've told you," he repeated, "I know nothing of it."

"Last week they ravaged Ipswich. Now they're at Maldon," and Gode pointed accusingly at the distant wood, "camped on an island in the River Blackwater."

"They must have moved on," said Godric. "Those seafarers are as slippery as eels."

Gode frowned fiercely and shook her head.

"Food," said Godric, "and some bandage for a hurt."

"Come then," said Gode curtly, and she turned and disappeared into the hut.

All this time, Edgar had stood silent. Now, sensing his chance, he said unexpectedly, "Can I have your spear?"

"You can look at it," said Godric, good-naturedly. He handed it to Edgar who turned the slender stem of ash in his hands, entranced. "I'll throw it," he said, raising it above his shoulder with some difficulty, daring Godric to stop him.

"Come!" called Gode sharply, addressing herself more to Edgar than to their guest.

The seasons of the day made little difference to the inside of the hut. It was a gloomy den, a single room with a hearth at its centre; there was smoke but no fire. Pungent animal-skins were stretched over the soil; there was a table, roughly joined, standing in one corner.

"Sit down," said Gode.

And Godric and Edgar sat down. They faced each other across the hearth.

Gode tossed back her pale hair, more composed now, feeling that events were under control; composed, and perhaps even glad to have something to do, glad to escape from herself. For all that endless, empty day, she had been prey to her own teeming fears for her father Dunnere. She looked questioningly at Godric. "Your hurt?" she said.

"Dunnere's doing fighting," Edgar announced proudly.

Godric nodded at Edgar, and he sighed. "Yes," he said. "I know." Then, turning to Gode, he said "It's here." And putting one hand over the other, he pressed his left thigh. "The horse threw me, and my spear's point gashed me when I fell."

Edgar looked interested. "Poorly," he said.

Gode dropped on one knee beside Godric. She saw how his clothing was stained dark with blood, how the cloth had ripped, then stuck to his torn skin. "It's bad," she said. And she was amazed she had not noticed it before.

"It could be worse," said Godric.

"I'll get some water from the well," Gode said.

"No," said Godric sharply.

Edgar's eyes opened very wide. He frowned at the tone of Godric's voice, and edged backwards.

"Is it far?" asked Godric. "I can't wait long."

"It's only across the yard," said Gode. "Edgar will talk with you."

But Edgar would do nothing of the kind. "Wait!" he called unnecessarily, and scrambled to his feet.

Then Gode picked up an earthenware pot and, with Edgar tripping over her heels, walked out of the hut.

Godric looked about him, at the worn sheepskins on the floor, the pans by the hearth; he stared at the gleaming wind-eyes, and at the larger smoke-hole in the roof. Then he leant back, pillowing his head on the palms of his hands, and closed his eyes.

The two children hurried across the yard to the well. While Gode turned the handle, paying out the rope, Edgar lay on his stomach and leaned over the edge; he peered into the darkness, and pitched little pebbles into the water.

Gode winched the bucket to the surface again; it swung on its long rope, banging against the sides of the well. The sounds it made echoed, and re-echoed.

Then, holding the pitcher under one arm, Gode slopped some of the icy water into it. "All right," she said to Edgar.

But Edgar was already making his way, not to the hut, but to what interested him altogether more: Godric's shield and spear.

"Leave them alone," said Gode without any conviction at all. For she too was drawn by the weapons, lying there in the dust. She had never seen such glorious war-gear: tempered iron, inlaid with garnets and gold, wrought by master-smiths. Half-drawn, half-meaning to restrain Edgar, she stepped forward, and knelt by the weapons.

Then Gode saw it; sharply she drew in her breath. She felt hot and cold, a tingling at the nape of her neck. "Blood," she said disbelievingly, as if her eyes deceived her. They did not. The shield and spear-tip were spattered with blood, blood still red, recently clotted.

"Poorly," declared Edgar.

Gode pushed him away. "Why?" she said. "Why blood?" And her own blood raced within her; her heart thumped so hard that it hurt.

She stood up, pouting as she thought; she wondered what it could mean, what it could possibly mean. A suspicion . . . she dismissed it. Once more Gode felt afraid. And she wished very much that her father, Dunnere, on this day of all days, was not so far from home.

Then she walked across to the great bay who looked at her with some interest. Her mind was confused; she leaned her head against its comforting warm flank. Her mind was confused: the blood, her father, his danger, her father, the blood, their danger.

Edgar knew something was wrong; he trailed behind Gode and presently tugged at her sleeve.

Suddenly the horse tossed its head and neighed. Gode started, and dismissed her thoughts. She smiled gravely at her brother, mindful of her responsibility for him.

"Look!" said Edgar, pointing with a stubby forefinger. "That's a saggle."

"What?" said Gode.

"Saggle."

"Saddle," Gode corrected him. And even as she said it, she

saw the eagle on it inlaid in gold: Byrhtnoth's eagle-sign, the emblem of the prince, leader of the East-Saxons. And Gode knew at once that this must be, could only be Byrhtnoth's, Byrhtnoth's bay; and she knew too that Godric must have fought and fled from Maldon that day.

A quiet rain began to fall then, a small mournful rain out of the iron sky.

Gode trembled with fear and fury. She trembled for her father, her father fighting against the sea-wolves; and she seethed with anger at Godric's treachery, his calm, his pack of lies. Now she understood why he had not given her his name at first; now she understood why he wanted food; why he had looked nervous when she said she was going for water.

Then, with shaking hands, Gode unfastened the girth and, reaching up, slipped the saddle from the great bay's back. She carried it into the hut. Edgar reeled after her, anxious and clutching the pitcher.

Godric sat up.

And Gode hurled the saddle at his feet.

She looked at him; and for a long moment he looked back at her, then he turned his head away.

"Godric," cried Gode. And then again, less fiercely, no less passionately, "Godric. Godric. You will live to hate your name as other men will hate it." She hardly knew what to say, there were so many things to say.

"It wasn't a fight," said Godric defensively. "It was a butchery. Byrhtnoth in his pride let the Danes cross the causeway from their island encampment; the Vikings waded across the shallow water. They outnumbered us. Five to one, six to one, they outnumbered us."

Gode looked at him with contempt.

"They shattered the shield-wall; those with horses were

thrown. I saw Wulfmær, Byrhtnoth's sister's son, slashed by the sword; corpses floated in the river; the water ran red." Godric closed his eyes. "And Byrhtnoth himself was killed, his neck was slit open. He cried to the Lord, then the heathens hewed him down. Girl, you do not know—"

"I know," interrupted Gode angrily, "that you've stolen your lord's own horse. I know about the oaths of loyalty." She gripped Edgar's hand and, small as he was, or perhaps because he was so small, he gave her greater strength. "My father has told me, told me the duty of every thane and churl. I know you must fight when your lord is slain. You must avenge your lord, or else lie dead beside him."

Then Gode burst into a storm of tears; her whole body shook as the full force of what she said dawned upon her. She wept for her father. She wept for her brother and for herself.

"Don't cry," begged Edgar. "Don't do crying." He tugged at Gode's arm; but it was no good. And caught up in this scene without fully understanding it, his own eyes brimmed with tears.

Godric looked at the pair of them uneasily. There was nothing he could do; there was nothing he could say.

"I know the fate of the coward," said Gode in a low voice. "My father told me. You may no longer own land, whoever you are; and you can have no lord, you must lay aside laughter and happiness."

Godric shivered involuntarily, unnerved to hear this girl, this daughter of a churl, tell him all he knew so well.

"For all your days you'll be a wanderer," said Gode. Then her voice softened a little; it was as if she was overawed at the thought, and the meaning of what she had said. "You cannot stay here," she added. "Food you can have, bandage you can have. Then you must go. My father is a man of two hundred shillings; you cannot stay on land he owns."

Godric looked at her with hurt and hatred in his eyes. She had wounded him more with her true words than any weapon could do, far more than the glancing blow of a Danish axe that same afternoon. "Give me the water," he said to Edgar. "I'll wash and bandage myself."

Gode gave him a strip of cloth; and, hardly knowing what she did for she was spent by emotion, she put aside for him a generous amount of food.

Then Godric stood up and, leaning forward, tipped the rest of the water in the pitcher over his head. He picked up the food after that and, limping a little, walked out of the hut.

In the yard, hampered by his wound, he struggled with great difficulty on to the horse's bare back. The children watched him in silence. Once more he sat astride the gleaming bay, the horse of the prince he had betrayed. He looked down at Gode and Edgar. "Thank you," he said grimly, "for telling me the way."

And with that he spurred the steed, and rode bareback out of the yard.

It was still raining softly, a sad rain from heaven. Gode and Edgar were once more at the entrance to their hut, in and out of which the hens strutted as inclination took them.

The horseman receded into the distance, heading across the blasted land, a rider with nowhere to go.

But Gode was already looking once again to the west, to the backdrop of the distant wood that stood before Maldon. Hopeless, she still hoped. And her brother Edgar sat at her feet, astride the gleaming saddle.

The rain quickened a little and then, quite soon, the curtain of that August day began to fall.

The Childmaster

And any man who loves learning is happy; and he who will neither learn nor teach when he can, slips little by little away from God.

*t*HE wind was blowing so sharp and cold that the storm
water hung in long spears where it ran off the roof of the
New Minster. Here and there on the flagstones of the cloister,
where the rain had been blown through the arches, it lay frozen
in clear sheets of black ice. Over the head of the boy-monk who
was walking in the cloister now, the storm moaned and howled,
sharpened to a whistle as it ripped through the stone wings of
the angels on the tower. The boy walked steadily, with a calm
face, his sandals clattering on the stone floor. He was carrying
a pile of clean linen towards the sacristy.

As he reached the eastern side of the cloister, beyond the
windbreak offered by the refectory, the gale seized his plain
black robe, wrapped it round his thin body, and cut through him
to the bone. It flapped the pile of white cloths in his arms, and
tugged at them. He held them tighter, and walked on. His face
was held stiffly in the same expression of calm.

Not his thoughts, though. He was struggling with himself,
the thin weak voice of his good angel arguing with the bad
angel, that always seemed the stronger.

"Why should I, why should I for *him*?" he was thinking. "Isn't it cold enough already? Did he ever have pity on me? Hasn't he beaten me often and often, for the smallest mistake? My bones ache at the memory of it, even in this cold. Why *should* I?" But when he reached the corner where the cloister turned and ran past the infirmary, he stopped. Brother Wulfstan, childmaster, lay sick there, and slowly dying. The boy stooped, and slipped off his sandals. He almost whimpered as he walked the rest of the way. The skin on the soles of his feet stuck to the icy floor, and smarted as he lifted his feet. But Brother Wulfstan was spared the clatter of sandals on stone.

In the doorway of the church he stopped, and put on his sandals again. The sacristan was waiting for him.

"Thank you, Brother Oswald," he said, holding out his hands for the altar-cloths. "Now help me with these candles."

The boy did as he was asked, standing with his arms full of candles, handing them one by one to the sacristan to set upon the altar.

"You will not be kept on such tasks as these for long now," the sacristan said kindly, as they finished. "The abbot has appointed a new childmaster." He waited for an answer, but he got none. The boy stood, sullen-faced, saying nothing.

"Off you go then!" said the sacristan, irritated.

Oswald went. As he left the church, and started back through the cloisters, he raised his eyes to the great tower, rising grandly into the leaden sky, seeming to topple against the racing cloud. He looked all round to make sure there was nobody within earshot to hear him, and punish him for breaking the rule of silence, and then said loudly, bitterly, "This weather reminds me of the day I came here!"

He had been in the cow-byre, trying to break the ice on the

water-barrel and draw water for the beasts to drink, when he heard his father calling. He left the ice unbroken, and went across the yard. His father and mother were standing together in the door of the house. His mother, he saw at once, had been crying. He heard his father saying to her, exasperated, "He has always been puny and slow. He has been sickly twice this winter . . ." But seeing him his father broke off, and said, "Get your cloak, son. You are coming with me."

"I will come too," said his mother.

"Where are we going?" he had asked, as they trudged down the track to the village, but he got no answer. He slipped his hand into his mother's, and she held it very tightly.

"Winchester," said his father suddenly, as though he had only just heard the question. Oswald had been there before, to the market, when there was a calf to sell, or a lamb.

"What have we to sell?" he asked.

"Nothing!" his father shouted at him. "Don't you know that? Are you too stupid to see what has happened? We have nothing left at all!" After that the boy asked no more questions.

They went through the market-place without stopping, and on through the streets of the town, till they reached the great stone wall of the New Minster. Rainwashed, gusty with wind, the streets were nearly empty of people, the windows were closed. At the minster the wooden gates were shut, and Oswald's father pulled a rope which rung a little bell.

"Think again!" said Oswald's mother suddenly, desperately.

"Would you rather we took him to the slave-market?" his father replied. A monk opened a porthole in the door, and looked out, blinking as the cold draught struck his face.

"We want to see the abbot," said Oswald's father. The monk looked at them doubtfully. Then he saw Oswald, hiding in the folds of his mother's threadbare cloak.

"I will ask if he will see you," he said. "Come in."

The windswept room in the gatehouse where they waited seemed warm after the gale outside. They did not speak, or even look at each other. Oswald wondered how anyone had managed to cut the stone flat enough to make so smooth a wall; the only building with stone he had ever seen in the making had been the drystone chimney for the neighbouring farmstead.

The abbot came. He was tall, dressed in fine robes of black, with a rope girdle, and a wooden cross hanging round his neck. Oswald's father said:

"We have brought our son to offer him to God."

The abbot took a long cool look at the three of them. His eyes rested longest on the boy.

"What are you called, boy?" he asked.

Understanding nothing, but frightened, feeling himself in danger, Oswald could not answer.

"His name is Oswald," his father answered for him. "He is nine years old next Easter."

"What do you best like to do, Oswald?" asked the abbot. His voice was kind.

"Oh, he likes to pray," said Oswald's father, hastily. "Often I have to shake him to bring him back from heaven, and keep his mind on his work . . ."

Oswald said, "I like to sing."

"That will do well enough, my son," said the abbot, smiling, taking Oswald's hand.

"Father Abbot, we cannot make an offering for his keep," Oswald's father was saying. "We are poor folk, and have no means . . ."

"I did not ask you for it, my friend," said the abbot.

But Oswald's father started again, like a man who has been interrupted in a speech he knows by heart.

"Father Abbot, we cannot make an offering for the boy's keep; we are poor tenants on the minster's land, and the famine has struck us so cruelly we have eaten even our seed-corn."

"Indeed?" said the abbot quietly, looking hard at Oswald's father. Then he said in an altered tone, suddenly brisk, "We cannot have our land unplanted. Go to the storekeeper, and tell him how much corn you will need for the spring sowing." Then to Oswald's mother he said, "Come with the boy, and speak for him."

The church was full of men in black robes, and full, Oswald saw, of little boys too, and they raised their voices, and sang, a strange song with words in an unknown tongue; and the abbot stood Oswald before the great altar, and asked him terrible questions: "*Do you renounce the world? Do you renounce the flesh? Do you renounce the devil, and all his works? And all his pomps?*" They did not expect Oswald to answer these things for himself. A monk at his elbow leant over, and said in a whisper, "Say, '*I do renounce them*'." And Oswald said it. Then they brought him a black robe to wear, and told him to say good-bye to his mother, and led him away through another door. He had not seen her again.

Sometimes his better self told him that his father had meant him good; that it had been meant to save him from famine. It was true that since he had been here, with the good plain food of the boy-monks to eat, his sickness had not returned. But most days he knew perfectly well that he had been sold in exchange for a bushel of corn to plant his father's field. And he could not forgive it.

From the first he had hated the minster. Yet he had truly said he liked to sing, and all day long the monks sang one service after another, psalm after psalm, in solemn process, sent heavenwards to find the ear of God. And the music they sang too was beautiful, but Oswald could not understand the words of any of it, knowing no Latin, and nearly every day his tongue slipped on some strange syllable, and he was beaten for his mistake. Over and over again the choir-monks explained to him that there must be no imperfections in a song offered to God. But he could learn better Latin only from the childmaster; and the child-master was Brother Wulfstan.

Brother Wulfstan was an old man and his lessons wandered. Often he spent time telling the boys about Dunstan and the other great men whom he had known when he was young. And for some reason he was unable to remember Oswald's name, but kept calling him Aldhelm. He would turn to Oswald, and ask him some hard question, getting his name wrong, and then he would become angry, and shake his head, and before long Oswald would be holding out his hands for a beating that made his eyes smart with tears. As for the Latin, Oswald learned very little. He was new, and all the others knew more, and Brother Wulfstan never stopped for him, or gave him any help. After a while he was forbidden to use English even to talk to the other boys in the short hours when talking was allowed; he still knew scarcely any Latin, and he became completely cut off, alone in an alien world.

Now Brother Wulfstan lay dying in the infirmary beside the cloister. There were no more beatings. Instead there were endless small tasks set by the monks to keep the boys from mis-chief. Now that the sacristan had finished with him, Oswald walked back to receive a new task.

Brother Edmund wanted him now. Oswald stood beside the reading-desk, and cradled a pot of ink in his cupped hands, keeping it warm by clutching it and blowing on it, so that it ran smoothly from Brother Edmund's pen. Lightly pricked out on the creamy parchment was a huge letter L ready for the splendid decoration with which the initials of a book were loaded. Brother Edmund dipped his quill into the ink between Oswald's fingers, and wrote LAUDAMUS.

"What does that mean?" said Oswald, forgetting that he was forbidden to speak English.

Brother Edmund frowned. He turned from his work to glare at Oswald. Then he smiled, a smile that made wrinkles run all over his face.

"When there is a new childmaster, you will soon learn more Latin, my son," he said. "I went to see Brother Wulfstan yesterday." He dipped his quill and wrote some more. Then, not looking up from the page, he said, "He is very sick. He tosses on his bed, and asks all the time for Aldhelm." Carefully he penned a flourish on the last letter in the line. "The brothers tell him again and again that Aldhelm is long dead; but still he gives himself no peace, but asks and asks."

Oswald said nothing. Brother Edmund looked at him, and went on looking. His eyes were difficult to face. Oswald hung his head. "He knows," he thought. "He has heard the lessons from where he sits writing in the cloister."

"Be off with you now," said Brother Edmund, irritated. Oswald put down the ink, and turned to go. Then Brother Edmund said, "*Laudamus* is the word you did not know. It means 'Let us praise'. Don't forget it."

Oswald, cheeks glowing with a shamefaced blush, made off down the cloister, to the church, joining the line of monks called by the bell to sing Nones.

He sang with all the rest, his voice hesitating while he listened what the others sang, and ringing out clearly only when the word was already begun. He tried not to think of Brother Wulfstan, but all through the service he was saying to himself, "Why should I, why should I, for him?"

"*Laudamus Dominum*," sang voices all around him.

The new childmaster was a long time coming.

"Soon," the choir-monks told the boys every day, smiling. "He has a journey to come. But he will be here soon." Yet the long weeks had dragged into more than a month, two, three months before he came. And all this time Wulfstan lay sick. He neither got better nor worse.

"His body is ready to go, but his heart is not," said Brother Edmund in Oswald's hearing.

When at last the childmaster came, he was a young monk, called Brother Aelfric. He smiled at the little group of boys, sitting on stools in the cloister. He was carrying a cane, but he did not keep it in his hand, he put it on the ground, and left it there. One by one he called the boys up to sit beside him, and asked them their names, and how long they had been in the minster. Then he wrote a few words on each boy's slate, and sent him back to his place. Oswald, lurking fearfully right at the back, was the last to be called. Brother Aelfric wrote on Oswald's slate also; then he said:

"The wind has dropped now, and the sun is warm. Pick up your stools, and we will go out into the open air. You are to learn by heart the words I have written on your slates; but you can do that just as well in the sun."

Brother Aelfric got up, and took a key from a bunch that hung at his belt. He opened a little wooden door in the cloister-wall that Oswald had never seen open before, and the sun streamed in through it. Beyond, was an orchard with long grass under the trees. The boys ran out, and scattered, racing each other to the far end, where the outer-wall of the minster bounded the garden. Oswald stood for a splendid dazzled moment in the doorway, looking out, watching the running boys, hearing them, as soon as they had gone a little way, calling to each other. Summer had crept over the land while he had been closed away, seeing only stone walls, and the square of sky over the cloisters. There were leaves on the trees, and swelling apples still green nestling among them. The light was dappled with shade; not the solid deep shade cast in great blocks by the minster buildings, but a soft and leafy shade that was delicious to walk in. Brother Aelfric called them all together and settled them down, sitting under the largest tree to work.

On Oswald's slate were written words in English, and beside them words in Latin. He set himself to learn the Latin. But the list of words brought sudden tears to his eyes, reminding him of home; *oxen, yoke, plough, share* and *coulter, acre, hay, water.* . . . That seed-corn should be green now, and inches high. Blinking fiercely to clear his eyes, Oswald set himself to learn.

For three days Brother Aelfric took them out into the garden, and gave them words to learn. For three days he did not beat any boy. From between the branches in the orchard Oswald could see the tower of the church rising into a blue sky. He could see the wall of the cloister warm in the sun, patched with moss, and haunted by butterflies. He got hot out there, and was grateful for the tall cool spaces when they went inside; as they passed the infirmary he took off his sandals quite willingly, for the flagstones felt cool and pleasant underfoot. He would have been happy if he had not found himself facing Brother Edmund across the choir when they sang, and felt himself still shrinking from those stern demanding eyes. Oswald was tired of saying "Why should I?" and feeling hot anger inside.

Then one morning Brother Aelfric gave them a different lesson. He kept them in the cloister, and one by one he made them stand up and speak to him without looking at their slates.

The oldest boy came first. Speaking slowly Brother Aelfric asked him, "What work do you do?"

"I am a monk," the boy answered, in careful Latin. "I sing all day seven times with my brothers, and I am busy reading and singing, but still between times I want to learn to speak the Latin tongue."

"Good," said brother Aelfric, "Good. Now Edgar, your turn. What work do you do?"

Edgar said, "I am a shepherd. I take my sheep to pasture, and stand over them, in heat and in cold, with my dogs, lest the wolves devour them, and I lead them back to the sheep-fold twice a day, and milk them, and make butter and cheese."

"Oswald, what work do you do?" asked Brother Aelfric.

Clutching the word-list on his slate, Oswald stood up, and began to talk about home.

"Dear master, I work hard. I go out at daybreak, driving the oxen to the field, and I yoke them to the plough. It is never so cold and rough in winter that I dare stay at home, for fear of my overlord." The words came tumbling out of Oswald, running into sentences as he remembered. "But I yoke the beasts, and fasten the share and coulter on the plough, and every day I have to plough an acre or more. . . ." He clenched his fists, feeling the hardened skin on his palms where the plough-handle used to wear the skin into blisters.

"What else do you do in a day's work?" asked Brother Aelfric, prompting him.

"There is much more to do. I have to fill the mangers with hay, and bring the beasts water, and clean the dung from their stalls."

"Indeed you work hard," said Brother Aelfric, looking at Oswald almost tenderly.

"The work is hard, because I am not free," said Oswald. And as he said this, suddenly he realized that it was all far behind him; he was a monk now. And a monk was a free man, living in a fine stone building, making and reading books, and singing, not sweating in the fields. He was a free man now.

Brother Aelfric was asking another boy, "What have you done today?"

"Many things," the boy answered. "Last night, when I heard the bell I rose, and went to the church, and sang Nocturn with my brothers. Then we sang the Litany of the Saints, and Matins, then Prime, and seven psalms with a litany, and the First Mass; then Terce, and High Mass, then we sang Sext, and ate and drank, and slept, and then we sang Nones; and now we are here with you, ready to hear what you say."

Listening, Oswald saw life stretching ahead of him in a shining vista of songs and books. He remembered home; the stench of the cattle, and the backache that came from ploughing, and the brutal anger of his father, and he was for the first time glad to be where he was. He smiled at Brother Aelfric, and Brother Aelfric smiled at him.

"You have all done well today," he said to the class.

Timidly, Oswald went up to Brother Aelfric, when the others were walking away.

"Will you take me to see Brother Wulfstan?" he asked.

"He is too ill to see you," said Brother Aelfric. "He tosses in fever, and asks all the time for someone who is dead."

"For Aldhelm?" asked Oswald.

"Yes, for him. How did you know?"

"He used to call me that," said Oswald, hastily, in case his courage failed him.

Brother Aelfric looked hard at Oswald. Then he took his hand, and walked with him round the cloister, towards the infirmary. All Oswald's fear of Brother Wulfstan came sweeping back, and if he had dared he would have run away; but he was drawn steadily onwards by Brother Aelfric's firm hand-clasp.

A fire burned in the infirmary, in a little iron basket, and the air was pungent with the branches of some sweet herb which had been cast into the flame to burn. Brother Wulfstan lay there, hair tousled, eyes looking wildly. When he saw Oswald he stretched out his wasted hands, and called out:

"Aldhelm! Aldhelm! At last, you have come at last! Forgive me, I did not mean it, I did not mean. . . . I told you harshly that you were wrong, and when you died there were cold words between us . . ."

"Brother Wulfstan, this is Oswald," said Brother Aelfric gently.

Brother Wulfstan looked at Oswald as though he had only just seen him. There was a little silence, and when the old monk spoke again it was in a quiet voice.

"Child, I was too harsh with you," he said. "You look so like him. It might be him that I see now. I loved him most of all the boys I have ever taught and loved. But he was not a monk. He went away to fight the Danes, and he was killed. So good a mind and heart to cast away. . . . That made me hard with you. But I am sorry for it."

"All right," said Oswald. He did not know what to say.

"And you are not content any more than he was. You, too, would like to go away. . . ."

"No," said Oswald. "I would like to stay here."

"Well, then," said Brother Wulfstan, in a suddenly fierce voice, "have you learned any Latin yet?"

"Oh yes," said Oswald.

He was going to tell Brother Wulfstan about the oxen and

the plough, but the old monk fell back on his pallet and murmured, "What can you say to me, Aldhelm?" His face looked strange as he said it, slack, undisturbed by the uttering of the question.

"*Laudamus*," said Oswald.

"Amen, amen," said Brother Wulfstan, seeming to fall asleep.

Thurkell the Tall

Then he was made captive, who before was the leader of England, and of Christendom. Then, in that very town from which the word of Christ first came to us, men saw misery where happiness had been. . . .

*t*HE nave of the great minster church was full of people. Women and children, townsfolk and black-garbed monks, were crowded into it. At the altar, standing alone, was the archbishop, clasping his hands in prayer, his eyes directed upwards towards the beams of the roof. All the doors of the church were closed and barred; against the great door under the west window the benches and kneelers had been piled up. And from outside came the noise of shouting, dulled by the heavy shutters on the windows and the great weight of the doors. Still there was no escaping the sounds of slaughter; terror sharpened the voices of victims outside to pierce the heavy oak and the impassive stone, and send waves of fear across the crowd inside. Then there were no more screams— only harsh brutal voices. And soon they began to batter upon the west door.

The low booming noise of the ram upon the timbers of the door rolled along the church, leaving silence behind it. With indrawn breath the great crowd waited—boom—for the door to give—boom—under the weight of the ram. With each resounding blow the great crossbolts on the door jumped in their sockets. In the whole church only the archbishop did not watch the door; he still looked upwards.

Then the slow booming stopped. There was nothing to be heard at all. The most horrible of all the sounds from outside was not more dreadful than that silence. Inside a woman began to scream. The scream was quickly choked off, as her husband put his hand over her mouth, and then the crowd waited hushed, as for the most holy moments of the Mass.

At last there came a different sound upon the door; many smaller thumps, scratching, and knocks. The Danish voices outside called to one another, and answered.

"What are they doing, ah, what are they doing?" whispered a young woman pitifully, looking to a choir-monk beside her. His lips were drawn so tight with fear that they were chalk-white. He seemed almost to be grinning, skull-like. He could not answer her. He was watching the door. Slowly the chinks of light between the two halves, and at the hinges, were being blotted out. Above the door was a fine window, double arched, with a round pillar to divide it. It was closed with a shutter of woven slats of birchwood, and now the points of light at the intersections of the slatting were suddenly exting-uished. On the right the shutter bulged inwards from something leaning against it. From outside there came shouts.

"Bal, bal, gera bal! Brenna!"

Someone cried out, "Fire! They are bringing fire!" And indeed, through the darkened chinks in the door faint wisps of smoke were drifting, curling. Screaming horribly the crowd stampeded to the far end of the church. They overran the precinct of the altar, and the archbishop, who till now had stood alone, was lost among them. The kindling that had been piled up outside leapt into flame, with a great roar like the sound of a river in spate. Smoke diffused in the air along the nave; high up the pale cool walls of stone it wound, snake-like, along the intricate linked arches carved there, and floated upwards to the painted angels on the roof. The stench of burning smarted in the back of men's throats. They coughed. Their eyes ran.

Suddenly a fierce light glowed upon the walls; the lattice in the window was a sheet of flame. A great tongue of fire was sucked inwards through it, and upwards towards the roof. Sparks blew in, and black cinders fell over the heads of the people. In only a few seconds the roof beams were alight. A great wave of fire swept along the church roofing it all with flame. There was no way out, for all the doors were barricaded. By now the fire had eaten through the timbers of the west door, but the great beams that had framed the door still stood, like the bars of hell itself, a black grid against a blinding sheet of flame. Then, with a noise like a clap of thunder, the west wall cracked in the heat, and a tumble of coping-stones fell from the doorway-arch.

It was a monk who ran first. He ran straight into the fire, flinging himself upon the blazing framework of the door, shrieking as he went. The charred beams were nearly eaten away; the trellis of burning wood collapsed as he charged through. Then there was a gap in the fire; one could see through to the open air. It was a way too terrible for most; but after a few moments another monk scrambled over the piles of glowing charcoal, and went running, with the hem of his robe on fire, on to the points of a bank of spears levelled to meet him beyond. Only when the roof began to fall in did the great crowd rush to follow him.

Outside the Danes lined up, swords and axes ready. They were in a blood-frenzy with the joy of victory, and they hacked down the terrified people as they ran out. There were survivors, nevertheless. Weight of numbers saved some of them.

There was no food in the town. During the weeks in which Canterbury had been besieged by the Danes, the townsfolk had eaten everything inside the walls, and the Danes had eaten everything outside. Hunger had made them savage when they finally broke through the walls; and when their anger had run its course they were hungry still. Parties of scavengers harried the surrounding country. The wretched prisoners were given no food at all. Soon one starving man bought himself a crust of mildewed bread in exchange for a betrayal; he told the guards that one of their prisoners was the archbishop, and pointed him out to them.

The man he pointed to was elderly, with grey dishevelled hair. His monkish companions clung to him, and wailed dismally as he was dragged away. His robe had been burned off below the knee, and he had lost one sandal. His features were pinched, and he swayed slightly on his feet as he stood.

"Are you Alfig, the priest?" the guards were asking, tugging at the iron fetters on his wrists.

Alfig closed his eyes, and collapsed upon the ground.

He woke to find himself in a cell in his own minster. A huge man, wearing the gaudy clothes of a Danish soldier, sat at his side. The man was stitching a black monk's robe, holding the needle delicately in great thick fingers. A little fire was burning across the room, with a steaming pot hanging over it.

"Who are you?" said Alfig, in a voice as feeble as a child's.

"You are alive then?" said the Dane. "There's broth ready for you when I've cobbled up the hole in this robe. Your own is not fit to wear, and he who had this before you will not need it again."

"Who are you?" said Alfig.

"I am Thrum, Thurkell's man."

"I almost thought I must be in Christian hands," sighed Alfig.

"Why, so you are. I have fought in England these twenty years, and have been baptized every time we were defeated," answered Thrum.

"Sometimes it softens your hard hearts," murmured Alfig. "Sometimes it makes good men, even out of Vikings. Olaf Tryggvason promised at the font never to come again, unless in peace; he kept his oath. I know it. Mine was the hand that baptized him. . . ."

"I would not remember him now, if I were you," said Thrum, sharply. "Come, take some broth."

But at first the archbishop could not swallow the food he was offered. The Dane sat over him, like a nursemaid, warming broth, and spooning it gently into the old man's mouth, a little at a time, till he had the strength to take more. For this purpose Thrum had stolen a spoon of silver from the strongbox in the sacristy of the church, risking a flogging from his fellows, for the army held all booty in common.

In a little while the prisoner recovered enough strength to pray; a little while more and he had enough to preach, gently but remorselessly exhorting Thrum to remember the vows he had made at his baptisms, and turn his heart to God.

Thrum said only, "I am Thurkell's man. Save your words for him." Nevertheless, he listened to what Alfig said.

When Alfig could walk, he was taken before Thurkell.

Jarl Thurkell, famous throughout the north for his great height and his great courage, sat drinking wine from a silver chalice that had been sacred to the blood of the Lord. He had established himself in the refectory of the minster, which smelt now of mead and wine and was littered with the weapons of his men. He sat in the archbishop's chair, with his feet propped up on the table in front of him, and looked coolly at the archbishop. A group of his men, with ale-horns in their hands, stood round him.

"We are glad to see you restored to health," said Thurkell, at last. "We hope for a great ransom for you."

From the archbishop's drawn and tired face a pair of pale sad eyes returned Thurkell's stare. "Has the King refused to pay you a Danegeld then?" he asked.

"Refused?" said Thurkell, laughing. "He was too frightened even to haggle. He has promised us forty-eight thousand pounds of silver."

"Yet you do not keep peace."

"He has promised, but he has not paid. We have to eat."

"Such a sum will take many months to find. The people will groan to pay it."

"When we are paid we will keep peace with him. In the meanwhile we will get a high ransom on your life."

"Where is the king now?" asked Alfig. He could not keep hope from lifting his voice.

"Safe, shut up in London. I do not think he will put his nose outside the walls till we're paid." Thurkell paused. Then he said deliberately, "He knows that we've taken you; that you're alive. There is no army on the march towards us; there's not even a messenger from him."

He watched Alfig closely as he spoke. The priest's face remained impassive; only a slight droop of his shoulders betrayed the relinquishing of hope.

"Why do you tell me this, Thurkell Jarl?" Alfig asked.

"That you may be the more willing to talk of ransom money."

"I have no money."

"But they say you are a holy man, sacred to the English god. A few words from you should loosen many purse-strings."

Suddenly the old man stood upright, eyes flashing. "I will not speak for myself. If the people offer it, that is another matter. I will not ask it of them. God knows what means the king will need to resort to, to raise what has already been promised you; I will not make the sufferings of the poor worse for my sake."

Thurkell looked at his prisoner, with interest, weighing him up. Then he turned to one of the men beside him. "Well, then, we will not need another place at the table," he said. "This old fool is of no more use to us than the rest of the captured rabble. Throw him back among them."

Slowly, with a sardonic grin on his face, the man Thurkell spoke to picked up an axe. Then, staring at the fire, he started towards it down the hall. Following his gaze, Alfig saw that a pair of wrist irons were ready in the fire, glowing. With a rag round his hand the man picked them up, and started towards Alfig.

The archbishop moistened dry lips with his tongue. "What do you want me to do?" he asked.

Instantly Thurkell got up. He smiled in triumph and contempt. He came down the hall, hands extended to his victim. "You yourself will know best to whom you must write," he said. "Come sit with me, and drink. I will see that my men respect you. You shall have a cell to yourself while we stay here; later I will do my best for your comfort. You shall have Thrum as a servant. Within the camp, do as you please; my word protects you. Only one word of advice; you are not my prisoner, you are the army's, for we hold all we take in common. It would be foolish to provoke even the meanest of them, for they have their rights. And if you think you may talk me into softness, as you talked Tryggvason, forget it. It would be rash to remind anyone of that story."

Archbishop Alfig sat down at Thurkell's table, and drank Thurkell's wine. Only, under his breath he said, "Christ pity me, Christ forgive me," to the brim of his glass.

The next day Thurkell came to the archbishop's room, two jarls with him, ready to ride, bringing parchment and a quill, and a jar of ink.

"Can you read English?" asked Alfig quietly, sitting down to write.

"I know what the word for money looks like, in English or in Latin," said Thurkell, grimly.

Head bowed, Alfig wrote:

In the name of Christ, by the obedience you owe me, his servant, I forbid any of you to give money for my life. But if any of you have money more than you need to live, for my sake give it rather to the poor.

✠ Ego ALFIG ARCHBISHOP ✠

He handed the letter to Thurkell. Thurkell found the word he knew, and was satisfied. Alfig wrote again. Then Thurkell's men went riding, one to London, one to Winchester.

Later the army moved to Greenwich. They had their ships there, and a camp with walls. The men made long huts to shelter in, by hauling ships out of the water, and turning them upside down upon tall posts. They made walls for the ship-huts out of wattle, and then a great number of men could sleep under each long-boat, dry and sheltered from the wind. The first night in camp Alfig slept under a keel like all the rest, but after that Thrum found a few wattles and made him a hut of his own. The hut was in a corner, right up against the earth-wall of the camp, and between two of the upturned ships. But it was not like the still cool cell at Canterbury; all day long the noise and bustle of the camp interrupted the archbishop's prayers and the Danes came to and fro past his door.

He watched them. The crew of the ship to the south of his hut were friendly. When the night was cold they brought him a brand from their fire to make one of his own; sometimes they brought him food. The men of the hut to the north were fierce. They never spoke to him, but they made the sign of Thor's hammer when they passed. They mocked and yelled when they saw others coming to visit him. They jostled Thrum when he brought water from the spring, and cost him many second 'ourneys. Sitting in his doorway, Alfig watched and listened.

One night the men of both ship-huts got together, and built a huge fire in the space between their two dwellings. They built it a good way off from Alfig's door, but he could see all that happened. They brought an ox, killed it, and hung it on a spit over the fire. Teams of them turned the spit all afternoon, while a captured English boy ran to and fro bringing water and ale to drink, for it was hot work, toiling so near the fire. The smell of roasting meat drifted on the air, as evening came.

When it was dark the men of the huts came to sit round the fire. They brought plenty to drink with them, and they had invited Thurkell's minstrel, keeping a place of honour for him, beside the fire. The minstrel sang to them, plucking a little harp to keep time to his voice. The songs were about Danish leaders, their battles and their deaths.

Finally the minstrel stopped. The men argued with him, voices raised. No, he would not sing any longer, he had to keep his voice for Thurkell's hall. He went off, with cries and catcalls following him, for it was early still.

And then from the darkness there came suddenly another voice, singing.

"It is the English priest!" said someone.

"Bring him, bring him!" they shouted, some mocking, some friendly. "Let's make him sing for us!"

Alfig walked into the circle of light around the fire, and sat down in the minstrel's place. Someone handed him the little harp. He struck a note from it. He sang them a song in English, in a strong sweet voice. They were astonished at his voice, knowing nothing of the need to set a great church ringing with the Mass. But they did not understand the words.

"Sing us something in Danish!" came a cry from the back. Alfig laid down the harp. Speaking a halting, careful Danish, he began:

"Once there was a lord who had twelve jarls. They had a journey to make across the sea, and they launched their long-ship when the sea was smooth, and the weather was fair. The twelve jarls took their places at the oars, and rowed the ship, but the Lord lay down in the bow, with his cloak rolled up under his head, and went to sleep."

They well understood this sort of tale. All round the fire they settled down to listen, turning towards him faces full of friend-ship, and eagerness to hear.

"But when the shore was left far behind, a sudden wind came over the water, and brought dark clouds, which covered the sun. The sea-birds flew away, going before the wind, and it was too rough to row. The jarls pulled in their oars, and began to bail water from the boat, but the waves grew higher and higher, and burst over the gunwales, and the wind roared furiously round them, and all this time their Lord lay sleeping in the prow. At last in great fear, the jarls went to him, and woke him, shouting, 'Lord, Lord, we shall be drowned!' And He woke up, and stood up in the boat, and stretched out His hands over the water, and said to it, 'Be still!' Then at once the wind ceased, and the water was calm, and the Lord lay down again and slept, but his jarls said to each other, 'Who is this, that the water and the winds obey him?'"

There was silence for a few seconds, and then a young Dane said, "It was Odinn, on his wanderings among men!"

Alfig smiled. "A god among men indeed, though not Odinn, but Christ."

"I should like well to serve a lord such as that, and have no fear of the storm," said another.

"He is a Lord who never turns away any offer to serve him. The weak and the old, the man without kin, even the man who has left his old lord dead on the battle field—all are welcome to the Christ."

Alfig paused. The Danes were silent, thoughtful.

"I have heard talk about serving a god before," said someone, suddenly. "It was a hard matter, full of deep thoughts. I would rather serve Thurkell, whose commands we all understand."

"The commands of the Lord Christ are not hard," said Alfig. "Like your own gods He demands that oaths be kept, that laws be obeyed. And to keep order in his lands as you do in your own lord's halls He bids you love your fellow men, even your enemies."

"That is a thing I would rather have my enemies do than my comrades in arms!" said a voice from the shadows.

At once everyone looked round, and those standing nearest

him moved to make way for him; it was Thurkell's voice. Standing outside the circle of firelight, he had been listening too.

Uneasily at first the Danes laughed. "Never fear, Thurkell, Tall-One!" cried one. "We will not love your enemies when it comes to the battle-play!"

"Ethelred the king is a good Christ-man, I think," continued Thurkell. "He loves us so dearly that he oppresses his own people to find money to pay us! He would rather load us with gifts of silver and of gold than raise a hand to hurt one of our number!"

At this the Danes laughed again, uproariously, while Alfig stood with a flush of anger on his face.

"And you too, priest," said Thurkell, "You, too, are a lover of your enemies are you not? Do you not beg your ransom out of the pittance of the poor, so that we may not lack anything while we are encamped in your land?"

Anger flashed in Alfig's eyes. For a moment it seemed he was about to answer; then he bowed his head. "Christ forgive me my weakness," he said under his breath.

"Bah!" said Thurkell, in contempt. "It is a religion of cravens and fools! And yet," he added thoughtfully, his eyes bent on Alfig, standing there with bent head, "were a man to take it truly to heart, it would ask more courage to follow the White Christ, than ever a Dane has needed to follow me."

He turned his back, and walked away. The Danes drifted away to their huts, in twos and threes, and Alfig stood alone beside the dying fire, head bowed down.

From that time onwards, Thurkell was more friendly towards Alfig. He sent gifts of food and wine, and even a psalter with a jewelled case from his share of plunder. Thrum told his charge

with clumsy kindness that this was a good omen; but Alfig knew
it was not. Thurkell now showed him the same jovial generosity
he used towards his men; he was a lord among them because he
fought more bravely than them all—he was generous to his
prisoner because he had triumphed over him. Alfig prayed every
day that Christ would pardon his weakness, would grant him
strength. And in spite of the gifts he grew thinner and sadder
day by day.

Meanwhile spring came. Primroses grew all over the steep
grass slope of the earth-wall round the camp. When Alfig and
Thrum climbed up to walk along the top of the wall they could
see bluebells in cloudy drifts beneath the trees on the landward
side of the camp. On the watery side, the willows along the
river broke into pale leaf and golden catkins, and the longships
lay moored in streams of silver where the river wound, shining
in the sun. Often when they returned to the little hut a party of
Danes would be waiting for them. First they came asking for
more stories, then for baptism, and service with the Lord Christ.
Lent was passing, and Easter was near.

At Easter Ethelred had promised the Danegeld. And it came,
on Good Friday, carried in heavy wagons, bound up in linen
sacks, to be carefully counted by Thurkell's jarls, sitting all day
at trestles set up in the middle of the camp, slipping it through
their fingers, weighing each man's share. They prepared a great
feast to celebrate.

The jarls were to sit with Thurkell, in the wooden hall that
had been built for him, and the men at tables in the open air. It
took them two days to gather enough food. On the morning of
Easter Sunday Alfig said Mass at the door of his hut, using an
ale-horn for a chalice, and a little wine Thurkell granted him.
Then he gave confirmation to Thrum, and seven other baptized
Danes. Then he shut his door, and stayed alone all day. The

camp was full of bustle, and beasts were roasting at every fire.

The feasting began at sunset; in the long pale dusk the sound of shouting and singing rose from a hum to a great joyful clamour. In Thurkell's hall all the leaders were gathered, sluggish with huge eating, and growing light-headed with drink. Outside the noise of the men grew louder; within nobody noticed. They all laughed, and boasted, and praised Thurkell.

"Oh mighty Tall-One," Olaf Haraldson was saying, "great glory and great wealth are the rewards of those who follow you. Your war-cunning is surpassed only by Odinn himself. You knew how to breach the walls of Canterbury; when the doors of their church would not give way, it was you who knew how to use fire to flush out rats in hiding . . ."

His voice trailed away into silence. Outside the hall the noise had risen to a clamorous din. Voices were raised in anger, there was running to and fro, and it was not the noise of revelry, but the howling of a mob out of control.

Thurkell's jarls got up, and buckled on their swords. The door was flung open, and in came Thrum, running, with a gash on his forehead, and blood trickling down his face.

"Thurkell Tall-One, come quickly, come now!" he said.

"What is happening?" said Thurkell.

"They are killing the priest!" said Thrum.

Thurkell scarcely waited to hear the answer. He ran down the hall, and out into the noise of riot.

The men were gathered in the camp yard. Alfig was standing on the platform beside the judgement seat, where Thurkell sat to settle quarrels. His hands were tied behind him. Howling with fury, the men of the army were shouting abuse, and pelting him with scraps of food and litter left over from their feast. Alfig faced them in silence, unshrinking, his head held high.

Thurkell thrust his way through the mob, bellowing at them

as he struggled through, and jumped up into his chair. A handful of filth aimed at Alfig showered over his head and shoulders.

"Keep quiet, you scum of all the earth, and hear me speak!"
yelled Thurkell.

At first it seemed he had made no impression, but very slowly
the angry voices died down, and, raising his voice high above
the continuing murmur, Thurkell cried, "Are you demented?
Do you not know this man is worth a king's ransom?"

But this question brought shrieks of rage, and another
shower of refuse falling around them. Then a man in the front
of the crowd shouted, "He has cheated us! He will not pay!"

"Kill him!" the mob howled.

"Listen to me!" cried Thurkell. "The money is late in coming perhaps, but come it will."

"He says it will not!" they answered.

"Pay no heed to what he says now; he has written, sent for
money to pay us. I, Thurkell, tell you so. I saw the letters myself, and myself dispatched them!"

And then Alfig spoke.

"You are wrong, Thurkell jarl," he said, loudly, triumph-
antly. "I wrote to forbid any man to pay money for me!"

The mob picked up the bones from the carcasses they had
feasted on, and hurled them at Alfig. Thurkell stood in con-
sternation, staring at the archbishop, and seeing on the old man's
face an expression of stern calm for the few moments before it
was masked in blood.

When he saw this Thurkell leapt forwards, and put his own
body between the crowd and its victim. His cheek was laid
open at once by a flying chunk of bone. Bleeding, he stood and
faced his men.

They stopped hurling things. They stopped shouting. A
murderous angry muttering came from a thousand throats.

"Step down, Thurkell, or not all the oaths we swore you will protect you!" shouted someone.

"He is our prisoner, Thurkell, not yours!" cried another.

"Then I will buy his life from you, at any price you like," said Thurkell.

For a few moments the crowd were silenced by surprise. In the hush Thurkell could hear the faint murmur of Alfig's voice behind him, saying "Domine, domine . . ." Then a Dane said, "No Thurkell, no!"

"A thousand pounds of silver!" cried Thurkell.

"No, no, no!" they roared at him.

"Ten thousand!"

"No, no, no!"

"All the plunder I have won this year!"

"No, Thurkell, no!"

"This year and last!"

"He has bewitched you, as he did Tryggvason!" shouted someone.

"All that I have," cried Thurkell. "All my tents, and all my jewels, my horses, all my slaves, two farms and a forest in Denmark, with cattle, with sheep. . . ."

"Even your ship, Thurkell," came a mocking yell. "Give us your ship too, Thurkell, and stay here to beg your bread!"

Thurkell stood silent, his face contorted with dark feeling.

"Your ship, your ship!" the mob were chanting at him. "Isn't he worth your ship?"

Thurkell did not reply.

"Stand down, then, stand down," they yelled, and, reaching up, they dragged him to the ground, set him upon his feet, and jostled him aside.

As soon as Thurkell was pushed away they began to pelt Alfig with stones. They made such an uproar about it that they did not hear Thurkell from the edge of the crowd crying, "My ship too, yes, even my ship!" Had they heard, they would not have heeded, once they had tasted blood.

When they staggered away at last to their huts and their fires, Thrum ran to the fallen body.

"You had best go quickly, now, master,' he said, and with the blunt end of his axe he made an end of it. Then he looked round for someone to help him carry the body. Only Thurkell was still there. Taking off his cloak, Thurkell laid it over the archbishop. Then stooping, he picked up the body by the knees, and helped to carry it away.

The next day the men were sullen, and shamefaced. They saw in silence Thurkell summon a party of Englishmen to take Alfig's body away. His voice stone-cold, his face impassive, Thurkell was like ice to everyone. But Thrum was busy. He went round the camp again and again, talking to groups of men in a lowered voice. At night he returned to eat at Thurkell's table. When this had gone on for some weeks, rumours about Thrum's talking began to reach the other leaders. Olaf Haraldson went to talk with Thurkell.

"You are playing a dangerous game," he said. "Are you resolved upon it?"

"Do you offer to come with me, Olaf?" said Thurkell.

"Not I. How long has this whim possessed you?"

"Since a man I had thought a coward turned out to be braver than I."

Olaf laughed. "Now if the White Christ can make a brave man out of King Ethelred, that will win me over too!" he said.

"All men have weaknesses," said Thurkell, tracing the outline of a ship upon the table as he spoke. "Farewell, my friend."

Three days after this Thurkell Tall-One left Greenwich. He

went stealthily, by night. He took with him many Christians from the army, and some of the old religion who were ready to follow him wheresoever he went. And he took service with King Ethelred, and swore to help him keep the heathen men out of his Christian land.

The Eye of the Hurricane

Then, when he dies, his lifeless body
Cannot taste sweetness, feel the sharpness of pain,
Lift a hand or be lost in reveries of the mind.

hAROLD lay under his shield. Like a dog he panted, the King of England, son of Godwin, son of Wulfnoth. All day he had defended Senlac Hill. He was the still-centre of the battle-storm, the eye of the hurricane. And his standard-bearers stood beside him. The Dragon of Wessex and The Fighting Man dangled, limp, uncrumpled. All day he had waited, given orders, prayed, waited. Again and again the Normans fell back from the brow of the hill. "$\overline{\text{Ut}}$, $\overline{\text{Ut}}$, $\overline{\text{Ut}}$", the English jeered and the Normans cried "Dex aïe, Dex aïe, Dex aïe."

Then through the silken evening air Harold had heard the susurrus of arrows, arrows, arrows, arrows. A shaft of fate rose and looped and swooped and struck him in his right eye. SCREAM. He screamed and wrenched at it with both hands, snapped it, snapped the shaft. Then the King of England moaned, and sank under his shield.

A vortex of pain, tearing pain, dragged him down. The pain, the lights, the dark, he spun. The whirlpool dragged him down and down. Giddy now, now floating, he began to dream.   He felt separate, separate from the raging pain in his body and the battle raging about it. They seemed distant, unimportant. His memories moved before him, years shuttered past in moments . . .

I was this year at Westminster Palace, in the King's Chamber; Edward, King of England, descendant of Woden, of the royal line of Cerdic. And the King was dying, slowly, dying. For the most part he lay motionless, and his face was white as a lily spathe.

I thought, *May you die, Edward. May you die soon.* Then I looked around at the others in the room: Stigand the Archbishop, Queen Edith and Robert the Breton, son of Wimarc. And they were all crossing themselves and mumbling prayers.

I pray you die soon, I thought. *I mourn your passing agony, I do not mourn your passing.*

And why should any Englishman? Year after year, and each year more, you have packed out the court with Normans, Normans, Normans. Schemers! Like weathervanes they turn and turn about, so that you are always behind them. Schemers, subtle and soft as cork. By God, may you die, Edward!

What did you promise William? What did you promise him? I know there's something spoken between you. What was it? Then I thought, *What does it matter? What will words count for now? If you promised William the throne of England, he will have to come and fight me for it. And if you did not . . . then also I think he will come and fight me for it. He will take for pretext the meaningless oaths he extracted from me in Normandy. What will words count for now? Either way he will come, we will fight. And either way, there will be Hardrada to reckon with, his limitless ambition, his flimsy claim to the English throne.*

But first it will be me, must be me. It can be no other. It cannot be little Edward the Atheling at this time. It must be a fighting man. Then ice will thaw; fair weather will return. Who will it bring first, William of Normandy, or Harald Sigurdsson of Norway? Brave warriors, sing your last songs as you sail over the swan's way. I shall slay you.

Edward, you detain us. What is there to detain you? Truthfully, nothing. Even your great edifice, St Peter at Westminster, is at last dedicated. It awaits you. That I will allow you: you have given a great abbey to the English people, greater even than my own foundation at Waltham.

Then you opened your eyes, as if you heard me. Those hooded lids peeled back, and you stared at me, and through me. And at your sign of life, all four of us stepped forward involuntarily, and the blood flickered in our frozen limbs. January, a stone-cold room: what a time, what a place to die, Edward.

"I have had a dream," you said, "a vision." And you spoke in a low, level voice that seemed quite disembodied, to have no connection with any living thing. "Two monks," you said, "stepped out of the darkness before me, and greeted me. I wished them God-speed, and at once they said: 'When you die, fiends will stalk through England for a year and a day; and they will harry the land from one end to another with fire and with the sword and with the hand of plunder.'" You paused, not flushed, not breathless, seeming not even to breathe. Then you said, "I told the monks, 'I will warn my people to repent. I will warn them to confess before it is too late.' And one monk said, 'Do not waste your time, O King,' and the other said, 'Your people will not repent and God will not forgive them.'"

Then you closed your eyes, as if to divest yourself of any further part in the thing. And I thought, *Your dreams, your visions—you would better have been a monk yourself. If there are any fiends in this land, O my king, they are disguised in Norman clothing.* And apart from Edith's renewed weeping, and the whispers of Stigand and Robert of Wimarc, it was as if you had not spoken. You lay as you lay before.

It was evening, the room was lit with candles, when you opened your eyes again. And again you looked at me. Then you tried to struggle up; you propped yourself on one elbow; you sat up. You were flushed, as if with wine.

We fell to our knees, all of us, beside your bed.

"Dex aïe!" you shouted. "Dex aïe! Dex aïe!" And hollow echoes of your words bounced back at you from the stone walls.

"Amen," I said. And the others said the same, "Amen."

I shivered then. I knew you were near the place where no one could go with you, where you could take only your own life for company—whatever that was worth.

"Dex aïe!" you shouted again.

"Amen, amen."

Then you lifted your right hand over my head, and you said in a loud voice, "Harold, you shall be king" . . .

Then Harold the King stirred; he panted more feverishly. His tongue hung out of his mouth, a pink thing set in a mask of congealing blood. Suddenly he shuddered, writhed, as if his whole body was a gathering, breaking, dying wave, a succession of waves, inconstant in their power, constant of movement.

He blinked the blood from the retina of his left eye. And he saw the battle around him, and felt part of it. He heard shriek and shout and scream; he saw his followers hold firm. He tried to speak, to urge them on. Then the words would not come. All men heard was a gasp, a rattle in Harold's throat.

Then the King saw his standards above him, The Dragon of

Wessex and The Fighting Man, floating now on the light evening airs. The gold, the crimson, then the blood-banner over all, crimson, crimson, crimson, black.

Then a house-carl came, and knelt beside Harold. He held his king's hand throughout his death agony . . .

"Eadgyth! You, you here? My love, my . . . Eadgyth? Is it you?"

"It is I."

"Is it you? I cannot see very clearly."

"It is I, Eadgyth."

"Ah! I knew you would come. You have always come when I wanted you, even though I never sent for you. That is how our love has been."

"That is how it has been."

"Let me look at you . . . Eadgyth! Eadgyth! How can it be so? Where are your years? You have thrown them away. You look as you looked when I first saw you . . ."

I remember that. I was just twenty-three, in my first year still as Earl of East Anglia. I had journeyed from Thetford with my shire-reeve as far as there was land to support our horses' hooves—even to the north of Norfolk, the mouth of the River Burnham.

The Burnham, yes, the same place, the same land my brother Tostig ravaged on his way north, when he joined forces with Hardrada. Tostig, may God forgive you.

It was my first tour; that afternoon, that spring afternoon we were at a mill, inspecting it. And you—there you were, your pale face framed in a dark doorway.

"Come here!" I said.

And you came, your long dark hair falling about you. You showed proper modesty, and yet not too much.

"Who are you?" I asked.

And you said, "My father's daughter," inclining your head to the miller.

"Not whose?" I said, "but who?"

"Eadgyth, my lord."

I thought—what did I think? I thought of a thousand things. You were so beautiful. You were so . . . my head raced like the water in the millstream beneath us.

How long ago it seems, long not in years but in events. How irritable I have been; how worn I have felt: strange, almost ready to die. It was not always so.

No, it was not so. "Come," I said, "Eadgyth!" And I turned to the shire-reeve and the miller. "Work is better-tempered with a little walking and a little talking."

And they bowed, poor men. What else could they do?

Then Eadgyth stepped out of the yard, and I said, "You lead, and I will follow."

So we walked until we passed a granary and jetties, and came to a bank, a great causeway that divided the salt-water and the saltmarshes from the fresh grazing land.

"Where does that dyke lead?" I asked.

And you said, "To the sea."

"Take me, then."

"But. . . ."

"Take me," I repeated.

We must have talked, but I cannot remember what we said. It seems almost like a dream now. The sun was dilated in the west, a great red eye over the River Burnham. You went before me along the top of the dyke, sure-footed, good in your movement.

There was such a great stillness in that place, a silence on which small sounds were embroidered: the call of a skylark, some distant shout, our own rare words.

Then something occupied that world, and it was no longer silent. At first I could not tell what it was; the air seemed simply to vibrate; there was no sound. And then a hum, an endless low hum. It grew, slowly it grew, until suddenly I knew it for what it was: the voice of the sea.

Eadgyth, you went before me, leading me on towards the sea. I thought of my shire-reeve and the miller, an hour behind us; and I gave them no more thought.

Then we were there. The water glittered, glittered, and the wind ransacked your hair.

I smoothed it back then. And you did not move, you neither flinched nor yielded, just waited, passive. And again the wind tugged, at war with your hair. "Swan-neck," I said. "You have a white throat."

"That is what they call me," you said, "Eadgyth Swan-Neck."

"That is curious," I said, musing.

"Why so, my lord?" you asked.

"I will show you," I said. "A little while, and I will show you."

Then we gazed together at the sea, the rocking flint-grey water, flecked with silver. It filled me with some great power and also with a great melancholy. Then I looked at you, and saw you were moved in the same way. "Our lives," I said, "are a day in the sea's life."

Solemn, you turned to me, and sloe-eyed. Then I took you in my arms, and you moved willingly to me. For a moment only, then you tore yourself away, roughly, and ran out across the sand.

I shouted, and followed you. "Eadgyth!" I shouted. And

there I caught you, at the water's edge, and you turned once more to me, laughing, and hurled yourself into my arms. Eadgyth! O Eadgyth! My first love, my love. · . . .

Then I said, "Eadgyth, I know you," for it was indeed as if I did know her, and had known her always, as if we had been waiting only to discover one another. And I said, "Come, I will show you."

Then we lay beside each other, out of the wind, under the shadow of a dune. And I threw back my cloak, and parted my tunic to show her.

"A birthmark," she said.

"It is," I said, "and is it not now and to you that I should show it?"

Eadgyth lowered her head, abashed.

"It is an S," I said, "the shape of a swan."

"It is," she said.

"I have shown it to no one, Swan-Neck. And to no one will I show it," I said.

"You have fine words," said Eadgyth.

Then I was seized with longings for her. My body trembled for her and I pulled her to me. I looked at her and my eyes burned with desire. . . .

"My eye, my eye, Eadgyth, it is on fire . . . my eye . . . I am burning, I am on fire. . . ." The King spoke in spasms, and in between he gabbled incoherently.

Then Harold screamed, and banged the blood-loosened earth with his head. The house-carl beside him called for a cloak. The bearer of The Fighting Man brought it and the house-carl gently slipped it under the king's head.

Night was close now. English against Normans, Bretons, Frenchmen, one for all and all for one—the dying Harold or the bastard William. Man against man against man against man. One jacknifed in agony; one marched on. Mace crushed helmet and head inside it, lance pierced mail-coat and heart behind it; one is one, all, alone, all, one. . . .

You take advantage of me, William. No man takes advantage of a Godwin for long. I know you now for what you are. What man would force another, to swear oaths under duress? They are meaningless.

"Harold," you said in your harsh voice, from your lofty, claw-footed throne. . . .

This is a charade. What is it for? Not to gain anything from me. You know that I am only acting. I would not swear these oaths if I were free, if I could escape your loathsome attentions in any other way.

". . . place one hand on each reliquary . . ."

How noble a mien; how ignoble a heart. You exploit sheer misfortune. As soon as word reached you that the warring wind and sea had swept me from my course, as soon as you heard that I had landed perforce at Ponthieu and been seized by Count Guy, your reaction was to calculate how to profit from it.

". . . and swear . . ."

So as liege-lord of Count Guy of Pontieu, you commanded him to hand me over to you. And you paid a heavy ransom for me, money and land. And how you entertained me—as if I was your honoured guest, as if I had intentionally put myself in your debt. What cunning generosity!

". . . that you will hold me as your lord . . ."

You have made no secret of my presence here. Not at all. You have proclaimed it, and showed me off in battle against the Bretons as if to boast: "What a man William must be to command such a man." William, how you patronize me. What gall you have to praise me for my bravery; and to present me with arms, me, Harold Godwinson.

". . . and swear that on the death of Edward, the King, you will further the claims of William Duke of Normandy to the English throne. . . ."

What can I do but swear? I say it is meaningless, yet no oath is meaningless, however it is made. God forgive me, I do not swear lightly.

"I swear these things," I said.

And William, Duke of Normandy, said, "Hold to them then. You have sworn on the relics of Rasyphus and Ravennus and many another martyr."

I shall hold to nothing. The time will come, in this year of grace one thousand and sixty-four, or next year, or sometime, when Edward the King will die; as like as not, he will confess himself away. But I shall owe you nothing, William. For all you have given me, you have given nothing with a friendly heart, and therefore I do not stand in your debt. Keep to your own land, and no harm will come to you; come to England, and nothing will keep me from you.

Then Harold lay motionless, he lay still as the world reeled about him.

Spear and shriek and shield and shout and sword and scream and scream tore apart the silken evening air. Hands and horses, helmets, heads were trampled underfoot.

And William cried out, William the Bastard hacked his way out; his horse reared over the dying, the dead, the dying. William cried out and the Normans fell back yet again from the brow of Senlac Hill.

Then Harold opened his left eye once more. He saw the bleeding eye of the sun and the ravens wheeling overhead, dark, crying for carrion. He thought then, *only the ravens will win.* And raising both arms in a gesture of defiance or else of submission, he cupped his hands and stretched them towards the skies. . . .

"Today," I said, "I mean to make a pilgrimage."

My brother Gyrth looked at me as if I had lost my wits. "A pilgrimage?" he echoed.

I nodded.

"You mean against William?"

"No," I said, "I shall go to Waltham."

"Waltham? This is no time to go to Waltham."

"I shall go," I said stubbornly. "William the Bastard can wait."

"Yes," said Gyrth. "And we must wait too, as you well know. Each day we wait, more men will join us. If we can stay in London for another week, even the most distant fyrds will have time to join us."

"That is true," I said.

"But you should rest," Gyrth said. "Above all, you."

"Why so?" I asked wearily.

"Why so? Don't you know your own limits yet? Three days back from Stamford, weary in flesh and spirit, and you talk of pilgrimages."

"I shall go," I said.

So I went, for I was eager to have one day of peace, one day away from the bustle of court, the preparation, the endless talk about William, William, William. And I knew that I owed God great thanks for my victory at Stamford against Harald Sigurdsson, and that I needed His support if I was also to defeat the Duke of Normandy.

Only two house-carls came with me; and, of course, my brave hounds—they ran before me, and their bells made fine music.

I rode north from London Bridge, out through the forest. Gyrth was right, in his own way. At once I felt weary, and my gout began to trouble me. I wondered as to the wisdom of the thing. I felt as if I could only endure the miles by setting myself against them. But then, after a time, the feeling passed; weary as I was, I found the rhythm of the horse's movement, of the day itself.

In the forest, leaves were falling steadily. There was no wind; they simply fell. I thought that the frost must have killed them as they quietly slept.

For mile after mile I was alone. I communed only with myself and with the world about me—the falling leaves, the grey-green trunks before, behind, around, the small pools with their ice wafers, the bells of my hounds.

The race north to York, and then on to Stamford, the great battle with Hardrada and with my own brother Tostig, the news of William's landing at Pevensey—they were all distant now. Far off, unbelievable. And the thought of what was to come—William, a second battle—well, let that be. That, too, seemed far off, far, far off, another world. *How*, I thought, *will the silence of this forest ever change? What has it to do with men?* Then I thought, *Men can change all things on earth. The Normans would want to hunt here with their hounds, they would hustle old men from their homes. They would give no thought to what my people need: wood for the fire, meat for the pot. There would be change, men would oppress and be oppressed. I fight that Englishmen can determine their own changes, and not have change—for better or for worse—forced upon them.*

So we came to Waltham, twelve miles out from London, and at last to the minster, my own foundation. And as I approached it, I prayed, as I always do, for Canute's kinsman Tovi, who first discovered the Holy Cross itself.

Adelhard and his canons were not expecting me. How could they have known that I was coming? But their welcome was none the less friendly for that. I walked in the precincts, talked with friends. This was my place; I felt happy.

Then, with Osgod, and Æthelric the childmaster, and with Thurkill, keeper of the vessels, and many others, I proceeded into the minster itself. I drew in my breath: the beauty of that place has always bound me with a spell: the great stillness within the great stone walls, the coolness, the glinting tapestries, the precious reliquaries, the silver and gold, the candles burning. And at the east end, Holy Cross itself, raised over all.

I threw myself before it. And I vowed: "O God, you granted me victory over Harald Sigurdsson; grant me now success against William of Normandy—I pray this in the name of the English people—and I shall give further riches to this foundation. I will endow it with great gifts, and with more land. And I will dedicate my life to your service."

Then I saw it; I saw it. I gazed at Christ on the Holy Cross, and in supplication stretched out my arms towards Him. Suddenly His head fell forward, drooped over me. . . .

Four Norman knights, unworthy of that name, burst through the circle of English house-carls still defending with their axes the body of their king. They hacked down Harold's standard-bearers, and the unarmed man at the king's side. The Dragon of Wessex and The Fighting Man were trampled and torn.

Then, shouting oaths, the four knights set about the English king himself. The first pierced his shield and stabbed him to his heart; and the second cut off his head; and the third drew and scattered his entrails; and the fourth, for want of anything better to do, hewed off his left leg.

At dawn the widows came. Dry-eyed, they stepped amongst the slain, each looking for one man.

And the two monks, Osgod and Æthelric the childmaster, came with Eadgyth Swan-Neck. They went about their gruesome task, searching for her loved one, Harold, the English king. And Eadgyth recognized her man because of their secret token, because of the birthmark of the swan.

Then William would not let them take Harold's body away. Not even in return for the dead man's weight in gold, willingly offered by his sorrowing mother Gytha.

And it was that Harold's corpse, wrapped in a purple robe, was buried under a cairn of rock within earshot of the sea.

"Buried," said William the Bastard, "buried by the shore he failed to defend."

Cold heart and bloody hand now rule the English land.